PUFFIN BOOKS

FLAME-COLOURED TAFFETA

Damaris Crocker had not lived her twelve years in smuggling country without knowing when a Run was planned. This night smugglers, or Fair Traders as they were known to the country folk, would bring more than just the usual contraband of brandy and lace. This night they would bring a mysterious, wounded, young man and almost enough high adventure, romance and danger into Damaris's life to make her forget the one thing she wished for more than anything else – a flame-coloured taffeta petticoat just like the one the gypsy girl had worn when she danced at the harvest supper . . . almost enough but not quite . . .

Rosemary Sutcliff was brought up in Malta and in southern England. She acquired a taste for history and historical romance as a child, and her novels and retellings have been widely acclaimed. She was awarded the OBE in 1975 for services to children's literature. She won the Carnegie Medal for *The Lantern Bearers*. Miss Sutcliff now lives in Sussex.

Other books by Rosemary Sutcliff

BLOOD FEUD

BONNIE DUNDEE

DAWN WIND

DRAGON SLAYER

EAGLE OF THE NINTH

FRONTIER WOLF

THE HIGH DEEDS OF FINN MAC COOL

THE LANTERN BEARERS

THE MARK OF THE HORSE LORD

OUTCAST

THE SILVER BRANCH

THREE LEGIONS

TRISTAN AND ISEULT

WARRIOR SCARLET

Flame-Coloured Taffeta

Rosemary Sutcliff

Illustrated by Rachel Birkett

PUFFIN BOOKS
in association with
Oxford University Press

PUFFIN BOOKS

Published by the Penguin Group
27 Wrights Lane, London W8 5TZ, England
Viking Penguin Inc., 40 West 23rd Street, New York, New York 10010, USA
Penguin Books Australia Ltd, Ringwood, Victoria, Australia
Penguin Books Canada Ltd, 2801 John Street, Markham, Ontario, Canada L3R 1B4
Penguin Books (NZ) Ltd, 182–190 Wairau Road, Auckland 10, New Zealand

Penguin Books Ltd, Registered Offices: Harmondsworth, Middlesex, England

First published by Oxford University Press 1986
Published in Puffin Books 1989
1 3 5 7 9 10 8 6 4 2

Text copyright © Rosemary Sutcliff, 1986
Illustrations copyright © Rachel Birkett, 1986
All rights reserved

Printed and bound in Great Britain by
Cox & Wyman Ltd, Reading
Filmset in Bembo

Author's Note

Anybody reading this book who knows the Selsey Peninsula will know that I have moved Carthagena Farm further south and changed it into the right kind of farm for the story (but the tradition that the old house was built from the timbers of a wrecked Armada galleon belonged to it from the first), that I have invented the village of Somerley Green and that I have played marshlight tricks with the run of the lanes and backways. But I believe that I have kept the spirit of the Manhood unchanged. I have tried to, anyway, because I love the sea-haunted land between Chichester and Selsey Bill.

Author's Note

Anybody reading this book who knows the Selsey Peninsula will know that I have moved Carthagena Farm further south and changed it into the right kind of farm for the story (but the tradition that the old house was built from the timbers of a wrecked Armada galleon belonged to it from the first), that I have invented the village of Somerley Green and that I have played marshlight tricks with the run of the lanes and backways. But I believe that I have kept the spirit of the Manhood unchanged. I have tried to, anyway, because I love the sea-haunted land between Chichester and Selsey Bill.

Flame-Coloured Taffeta

Rosemary Sutcliff

Illustrated by Rachel Birkett

PUFFIN BOOKS
in association with
Oxford University Press

PUFFIN BOOKS

Published by the Penguin Group
27 Wrights Lane, London W8 5TZ, England
Viking Penguin Inc., 40 West 23rd Street, New York, New York 10010, USA
Penguin Books Australia Ltd, Ringwood, Victoria, Australia
Penguin Books Canada Ltd, 2801 John Street, Markham, Ontario, Canada L3R 1B4
Penguin Books (NZ) Ltd, 182–190 Wairau Road, Auckland 10, New Zealand

Penguin Books Ltd, Registered Offices: Harmondsworth, Middlesex, England

First published by Oxford University Press 1986
Published in Puffin Books 1989
1 3 5 7 9 10 8 6 4 2

Printed and bound in Great Britain by
Cox & Wyman Ltd, Reading
Filmset in Bembo

Contents

Author's Note

Chapter 1: 'Spanish Ladies' 1

Chapter 2: In which Damaris finds her
Smuggler 13

Chapter 3: The Wise Woman 22

Chapter 4: Skills and Remedies 31

Chapter 5: Tom Wildgoose 40

Chapter 6: The Oilskin Packet 50

Chapter 7: Mr Farrington's Hunting 57

Chapter 8: The Wicked Thing 66

Chapter 9: 'Dame's Folly' 74

Chapter 10: His Majesty's Customs 82

Chapter 11: A Time for Parting 99

Chapter 12: Voices in the Waggon Shelter 101

Chapter 13: Wish on a Shooting Star 110

Chapter 1: 'Spanish Ladies'

The little lost cottage in the woods by Denman's Rife had been empty and hearth-cold so long that nobody remembered it was there at all. Its one earth-floored room had still the remains of a hearth in it, and at the hearth end, ragged wings of thatch still clung to the weather-rotted rafters, making a kind of rough shelter; but save for the wind-stunted oak and crack willow and hawthorn that crowded it round and linked branches above it, the other end, the doorway end, had no roof at all.

But last summer Damaris Crocker from Carth- agena Farm and Peter Ballard from the Vicarage, who knew the woods better than almost anybody except Genty Small the Wise Woman, had found it when they were looking for a badger's holt. They had taken it for their own, and furnished it with an old blanket and some candle ends and a couple of cast-off cooking pots and the like; and so the place had a kind of secret life of its own again, sometimes even a small fire on the hearth, carefully chosen and laid to make no telltale smoke. Also it had a name—two in fact—for Damaris had instantly called it Joyous Gard after Sir Lancelot's castle in the big brown leather book called *le Morte d'Arthur*, at home, while Peter who considered that too romantic called it Tumbledown.

This spring it was giving shelter to an injured vixen, penned there until her paw, caught in a trap, should be mended enough to let her go. Mrs Ballard at the Vicarage would never have given her houseroom because of her smell, while John Crocker, being a farmer and in the midst of the lambing season at that, looked on all foxes as enemies. So Damaris and Peter had her safe in the ruined cottage, and visited her as and when they could.

Damaris had just been there, with a bag of household scraps hidden under her dark green cloak, and fed the little vixen and refilled her water bowl from the spring nearby, and looked at her paw, which was healing nicely. It was Peter's turn really, but, though he was at home because of some fever that had closed the school in Chichester where he was a weekly border, he was, greatly to his disgust, having to do extra Latin with his father; and anyway, Aunt Selina had sent her to take a clutch of ducks' eggs to old Mrs Farrington at the Big House, and the two trips were easily combined if you took the old halflost track through the woods instead of going round by the lanes.

Snowball, her fat white pony standing patiently where she had left him hitched to a goat willow beside the track, swung his head and whinnied softly

2

in greeting. Damaris whinnied softly back—she could whinny quite well, well enough to satisfy Snowball, anyway—and unhitched him, loosing a cloud of catkin-pollen yellow as sunshine over them both; and leading him to the nearby oak stump that made a convenient mounting block, climbed into the saddle and headed for home.

Where the track climbed up into a narrow lane, she reined in for a moment and sat looking northward. She loved the view from that spot, where the land rose a little, across the farmland and the trees of the Manhood and the wandering inlets of the sea, to where Chichester Cathedral spire rose against the wave-lift line of the Downs. She loved that view in any weather and at all times of year, but most of all on a day like this one, under wide, sweeping March skies, broken sunlight and shadow drifting across the still bare woods, and the Cathedral spire coming and going as the light changed.

And as she sat there, she heard far away down the lane, the sound of a fiddle; and the fiddler playing a tune she knew well. Nearer and nearer it drew, and then round the corner from the direction of the village came the tatterdemalion figure with a patch over one eye, of Shadow Mason, his fiddle tucked under his chin, weaving from side to side, and playing as he went.

Damaris sang the familiar words inside her head:

'Farewell and adieu to ye fair Spanish ladies,
 Farewell and adieu to ye Ladies of Spain,
 For we've received orders to sail for old England,
 And perhaps we may never more see you again.'

Shadow Mason was an old sailor who had served fifteen years in the Royal Navy and lost an eye fighting the French long ago. Maybe that was why he

seemed to like 'Spanish Ladies' better than all the
working chanties that helped forward the work of the
merchant ships. The King's ships, he had once told
Damaris, did not need chanties because having a
fighting crew on board, they had enough men to
handle the sails and capstan without.

> 'We'll rant and we'll roar, like true Bri-hitish
>   sailors,
> We'll range and we'll roam far over salt seas,
> Until we strike soundings in the Channel of old
>   England,
> From Ushant to Scilly is thirty-five leagues.'

He always played that tune whenever he was
drunk, and almost always with that odd break like a
hiccup, somewhere in the chorus.

He was past her now, and weaving his way on
towards Itchenor. Damaris sat listening while the
tune faded into the distance.

> 'The first land we made, it was known as the
>   Dodman,
> Next Rame Head off Plymouth, Start, Portland
>   and Wight
> We sailed past Beachy, past Fairlight and
>   Dungeness,
> And then we bore up for. . . .'

She shook the reins and turned Snowball's head for
home.

The farmhouse of Carthagena sat long and low and
companionable in the first fading of the March
twilight, sideways on to the lane and separated from
it by a low flint wall, and a tamarisk hedge that tossed
and streamed like a breaking wave where the wind
blew through it. Damaris passed the hedge with its
gate into the narrow front garden where the first half-
wild daffodils were in flower, and turned into the

4

steading yard beyond.

Caleb Henty the horseman came out at the sound of Snowball's hooves on the cobbles, and lifted her down from the pony's back. That was when Damaris, pausing to watch them go while she shook out her bunched-up skirts, saw the cross chalked on the stable door.

She had not lived all her twelve years in smuggling country without knowing what that meant. There was a Run on tonight; need for horses to serve as pack beasts and mounts for the escort riders taking the cargo inland to the hides for safe storing until they could be got away to London town.

A little cold thrill of excitement ran through her.

John Crocker her father did not hold with smugglers or smuggling, but he always left the stable door unlocked on nights when the chalk cross appeared on it. Better that than risk having the stable fired with the horses inside it. Damaris could not believe that Caleb—who generally came to work looking as though he had not been near his bed on mornings after a run—would fire the stable with Daisy and Dolly and Beauty and Swallow and Snowball and the rest inside it, but her father said it was not just their own people: men came from far away inland to take charge of the pack-trains. So he left the stable door open and asked no questions, and in the morning Daisy and Dolly and the others would be there, mired and weary but perfectly safe. Sometimes a keg of brandy, too, by way of payment, though John Crocker always handed that straight over to the authorities. Snowball was never taken: he was too small and maybe he would show up too clearly, even in the dark.

Little brown Caleb, plodding across the steading yard with Snowball nuzzling at his bowed shoulder, began to whistle absent-mindedly

> 'Farewell and adieu to ye fair Spanish ladies,
> Farewell and adieu. . . .'

And something opened with a small soft click in Damaris's head, so that suddenly she knew what she had never guessed before: that Shadow Mason playing 'Spanish Ladies' in the lane, with that odd hiccup in the chorus, and the chalk cross on the stable door were part of the same thing.

Caleb broke off in his whistling, as though suddenly noticing what he did, and turned in the stable doorway to call back to her scoldingly, 'Ged 'long wid 'ee now, Mess Damares, ye'll be late for supper else, an' Company in t' parlour, too.'

'Who, Caleb?'

'Mus' Aylmer.'

'Mr Aylmer's not company,' Damaris told him. Luke Aylmer was farm bailiff to young Mr Farrington at the Big House, and when he came to talk over farming matters with Father he would often stay on to eat with them afterwards. But she hitched up her basket and scurried across to the narrow archway that gave onto drying green and dairy yard and kitchen door, untying the neck strings of her cloak as she ran.

She did not say anything about the chalk cross or the fiddle tune, at supper in the candlelit parlour, for another thing she had learned during her twelve years in smuggling country was that one did not talk about such things. Anyhow, she had been well brought up and knew about not speaking until she was spoken to, at least in company, even when the company was Mr Aylmer, who scarcely counted as company at all. And that evening Mr Aylmer was still busy talking farming matters with Father, and only spoke to her once. That was just about the time they had finished with the brace of ducks and Father was carving the leg of mutton while Aunt Selina who kept house for them, cut the raised pie, and in a lull in the farm talk Mr Aylmer turned to her and said, 'Well, Mistress Damaris' (He always called her Mistress Damaris, as though she were grown up: it was one of the things she liked about him, along with his round cheerful face and the beautifully curled wig he always wore over his own short red hair in church on Sundays.) 'Well, Mistress Damaris, you look as though you'd been out in the woods looking for the spring time; aye, and you look as though you'd found it, too.'

'I found five primroses in the ditch by Woodhorn Crossway,' Damaris told him.

'And I hear young Ballard is home while his school is closed with measles or the like. That'll please you—and him too, I reckon. Young things shouldn't be kept close-penned in school with the spring coming on.'

'Yes, but he's having to do extra Latin with his father.'

Mr Aylmer shook his head. 'That'll not please him; but I suppose if he's to follow his father into the Church . . .

'He doesn't want to. He wants to be a farmer,' Damaris said; and then rather wished that she had not, because she and Peter did not generally go round telling each other's private business to other people.

Her father put another large slice of mutton on Mr Aylmer's plate, and said, 'And sure enough he'd make a better farmer than ever he will a parson.'

'Oh aye, comes up and gives you a hand here at Carthagena, I was hearing.'

'When he gets the chance—at harvest time and lambing. Holidays and weekends and when school has the measles. He's got a real feel for the land.'

They had forgotten Damaris, and began discussing the prospects for the lambing season.

But Damaris had caught the faint note of regret in

her father's voice when he spoke of Peter having a feel for the land; and watching his nice bony wind-burned face with the fine crinkles round his eyes, while she ate her own pie, she felt, as she sometimes did, a little guilty that she was not a boy to carry on farming Carthagena after him.

But though she did not speak of them, she went on thinking about the fiddle tune and the chalked cross off and on all evening. And when she had gone up to her little room under the eaves, and undressed for bed, and kind fat Aunt Selina had come surging upstairs to hear her prayers, and surged away again taking the candle with her, she slipped out of bed again and, crossing to the small pale square of window, opened it and leaned out. The chill of the March night whispered through her white cotton nightgown, and she shivered, but the shiver was not really for the cold.

She could see out across the dipping roofs of the steading yard, and the open level of South Field, where Caleb had been at the spring ploughing with Daisy and Dolly that day, the trees of the Manhood dark in the starlight. The Main Wood, people had called it once, the dense fleece of woodland covering the broad tongue of land that reached south of Chichester into the sea at Selsey. Now it was cut up by farmland spreading from the coastwise villages until in places it was just pockets and patches and wild-duck streamers of wind-shaped oak and elm and hawthorn and willow. But still the whole district was called the Manhood, and still it had, at least for Damaris, a kind of magic about it.

It was looking very magical now, very still under the stars, for the wind of the early evening had quite died away. But the Manhood was only waiting: it would be busy enough later on, in its own secret way. Somewhere off-shore a lugger would be lying at anchor, and the small shallow-draught boats would be coming ashore with kegs of tobacco and French brandy and Holland's gin, and maybe bales of silk or cases of tea to be loaded onto the waiting horses. And presently the laden pack-train with their escort riders would be trotting away into the dark.

Damaris turned her thoughts carefully away from the Run, to look up at the stars over the Manhood. It was the stars really that had brought her to the window, despite the tune of 'Spanish Ladies' running in her head. If you could count seven stars for seven nights together, and then you made a wish, your wish was sure to come true. It was surprising how hard it was to do, because you hardly ever got seven clear nights in an unbroken string. But this time the nights had held clear, and the stars of this seventh night were hanging bright above the trees with no more than a wisp of cloud here and there among them. One bright star hung low over the great elm tree at the corner of Dinder Meadow; a small but diamond-blue star lower still, so low that it might have been a sea light. On second thoughts perhaps it *was* a sea light, so she let that one go, just to be on the safe side, and chose another, a little higher up. There were plenty to choose from, so she chose with care, as she might have chosen small wayside flowers for a nosegay. A soft rather fuzzy looking star all by itself in the mid heaven; another that shook clear of the barn roof even as she looked, as though it had come hurrying to be included. That made four. Damaris left the south-ward facing window and went to the little corner window at the foot of her bed that faced westward over the moss-cushioned roof of the brew-house and into the heart of the big mulberry tree that hung its branches out over the lane.

She picked her last three stars through the still bare branches of the mulberry tree, from where they hung above the creeks and inlets of Chichester Harbour. Then she covered her face with her hands very much as though she were saying her prayers in church, and wished with all the strength of wishing that was in her, for a flame-coloured taffeta petticoat.

Rather a small wish, seemingly, to make so much of, but Damaris had made it whenever she sneezed before breakfast or met a piebald horse or saw one of the shooting stars that sometimes arched over the Manhood on winter nights, ever since the gypsies had come, more than two years ago. That had been at harvest time, and she had been allowed in to the Harvest Supper in the great tithe barn, though it was long past her bed-time, and a gypsy girl in a flame-coloured petticoat had come and danced on the raised threshing floor in the midst of the place, to the fiddling of a little brown man with very white teeth who had taken his battered hat round for pennies afterward. Other people might only have seen a gypsy with bright eyes and brown flickering feet, dancing in a bright petticoat that was dirty and draggle-tailed. But Damaris had seen joy itself dancing among the corn sheaves in the leaping and flickering light of the lanterns and the stars beyond the great high wagon doorway that seemed to be dancing too. And that was what she still remembered even now that she was more than two years older.

But nobody understood, not Father nor Aunt Selina, nor even Peter who understood most of the things she told him. '*Girls!*' Peter had said, and Father and Aunt Selina had laughed kindly and said that it was a foolish fancy and a flame-coloured petticoat would be quite unsuitable for a little girl. So she had never mentioned it again, but she had gone on wishing for the thing which to her somehow stood for all the joy and laughter and beauty and shine of the world.

Her mother would have understood, the mother who had insisted when she was born on giving her the beautiful old Puritan name of Damaris to make up for having a surname like Crocker. But her mother had died so long ago that Damaris could scarcely remember her now.

She left the window and dived into bed, pulling the blankets to her chin and curling up like an earwig.

Usually she fell asleep at once, but tonight she lay awake for a long time, listening to the sounds of the old house settling for its own sleep round her. On stormy nights Carthagena seemed to remember the time when its timbers had been part of a Spanish galleon wrecked on the coast nearby as the great Armada drove up-channel; but on quiet nights it seemed to remember back beyond that, to the time when they had been part of a forest, and then it would settle as a tree settles into its own roots and the ground that it has grown from, giving shelter as a wide-branched tree gives it, to all its living things, not only to its humans, but to its beasts in the nearby steading yard, to True the yard-dog and Sukie the tabby cat, to the mice behind the wainscot and the bats in the roof and the swallows who had their nests under the eaves in summer . . .

The church clock, which you could hear on still nights or when the wind was in the right direction, struck ten, and she was still wide awake when she heard the hoot of an owl, and then faint sounds from the direction of the steading yard; a voice speaking at half breath, and the stealthy creak of the stable door, and the muffled clop of horses' hooves on straw-spread cobbles. No sound from True; all the Manhood dogs knew better than to bark at the night-time comings and goings of the Fair Traders. The owl cried again, and in a little the night was as quiet as it had been before.

11

Inside her head in the darkness, Damaris could see the horses being led down the lane between over-arching thorn trees, away into the open levels; Marsh Farm way, maybe. Saw them waiting among the dunes for the boats to come in . . . Little ripples of sleep began to lap around her, like the incoming tide lapping at the dune grasses . . . She did not know how long she had been asleep, when she was suddenly awake again and listening for whatever it was that had woken her. In a few moments it came again. She had heard it once or twice before, and she knew what it was, the sharp spatter of pistol shots a long way off.

Chapter 2: In which Damaris finds her Smuggler

The Horseman was by custom the earliest astir of anyone on the farm, for the horses needed to have their first feed of the day at half-past four, if they were to be ready for work by half-past six. But on the morning after a Run both Caleb and Dick Nye, the second horseman, and the Carthagena horses were generally somewhat late, and on this particular morning Damaris, who usually arrived at the stable to bid good morning to the horses only just before they were led out, was early.

It had taken her some time to get to sleep again last night, and she had woken well before daylight, remembering that distant spatter of pistol shots, and worrying about possible harm to Caleb or anyone else she knew. She had got up quickly, ignoring the flowered china basin and jug of cold washing water in the corner, huddled on her clothes, dragged the comb three times through her curly brown hair in such a hurry that she broke one of its teeth, and gone flying downstairs and out by the narrow drying green into the steading yard.

The first silver-gilt wash of morning was just beginning to lighten the sky behind the granary roof while the cart-shelter beneath it was still a cave of darkness, and the dunghill cock who always roosted on the shafts of the haywain was crowing as though it was only because of him that the day was coming at all. The first babble of lambs was coming over the wall from the barn fold, and Sukie who always grew very loving when she was going to have kittens came wreathing and purring round Damaris's ankles. Damaris stooped to stroke the little hard furry ball of the cat's head that thrust into the hollow of her hand. A gleam of lantern light was spilling out from the stable door. She pushed the door further open and went in, Sukie still weaving round her. The dim gold of the lantern light met her kindly on the threshold, and the good sweet breathy smell and the contented sounds of the stable; and she saw the big round rumps of the horses, their tethered heads lost in the shadows.

Above the thick warm stable smells, her nose caught the sharper accent of elecampane. She knew about that. Caleb was not like Matthew Binns, the head groom at the Big House—a horse-master possessed of the ancient skills, the magic of the toadbone and the words of power that could gentle a wild horse or drive a gentle one to instant frenzy; but none the less he was wise in most things that had to do with horses and their welfare, and he always scattered leaves of elecampane, fresh or dried according to the time of year, among the hay and beans in the manger of any horse that he thought might be too tired to eat up otherwise. There was something about it that they could not resist.

Caleb himself was at the other end of the stable giving a hurried grooming to Swallow, her father's riding horse, who swung his head and ruckled softly down his nose in greeting as she came up. But Caleb went steadily on with the curry-comb, hissing through his teeth the while. Dick Nye was safely out of the way for the moment: she could hear him in the harness room, whistling as he got down the day's working gear.

'Caleb,' she said, 'I heard something last night.'

'Did 'ee now?' said Caleb said, breaking off his hissing but still concentrating on the curry-comb.

'Yes I *did*.' Damaris kept her voice down: she had not forgotten that she should not be speaking about such things at all, but she was too anxious just now to worry about that. 'And it sounded like pistol shots.'

'Twouldn' be the first time anyone's heard pistol shots in the Man'ood,' said Caleb.

'I was afraid—is anyone hurt?—Anyone of ours?'

'Not as I knows on.' Damaris gave a small sigh of relief, and turned to Snowball next door, who was nuzzling at her, demanding notice and the bit of apple or carrot that she always carried for him. In contrast with Caleb and the farm horses, and even Swallow, who had all a weary look about them, Snowball had, as usual, clearly passed an undisturbed night and was fresh as a daisy as well as being as white as one.

'Now get 'long back to breakfast, will 'ee,' said Caleb, 'for I've enough to do, if we're to harrow Dinder Meadow today, wi'out you underfoot.'

Dick was coming in from the harness room with the great horse-collars on his shoulder. And she knew that there would be nothing more to be got out of Caleb anyway, so she went.

After breakfast Damaris did lessons for an hour and a half with Aunt Selina in the parlour: reading, sometimes from an improving work on etiquette for the young, sometimes from the Bible, but just at present from a new book called 'Pamela' by a Mr Samual Richardson; then writing, in a fair copperplate hand from the book they had just been reading, and arithmetic, which took the form of helping Aunt Selina with the household accounts, which would never have got done otherwise, for Aunt Selina had no head for figures, being more of a romantic turn of mind. (Damaris could still remember the twitter she had been in and how she had embroidered white roses on a scarf for Prince Charles Edward Stewart, him they called Bonnie Prince Charlie, when he had made his bid for the English throne five years ago, all ready to present to him when he got as far south as Chichester. Only of course he never did. But Aunt Selina still drank her mid-morning glass of elderflower wine in secret to 'the King over the water' and felt deliciously daring while she did it.) And then she had to spend half an hour working on her sampler on which a very sad poem beginning 'When I am dead and laid in dust' was surrounded by a border of pinks and honeysuckle and small stiff birds. And after that Aunt Selina found so many tasks for her in the still-room and the dairy that on this particular day it was noon and dinner-time before she was finished.

Indeed she might not have got away even after dinner, but she made an urgent excuse about Snowball needing exercise, and slipped out to the stable with the bundle of household scraps that she had collected earlier and hidden behind the brushwood pile, safe under her clock. She was quite used to saddling her own pony, for there was only Caleb and Dick to see to the horses, and they would be out harrowing Dinder Meadow and Church Mead until well into the afternoon.

She saddled up—she still rode astride with her skirts bunched to her knees, though Aunt Selina had begun to bleat that it was high time she learned to ride side-saddle like a lady—and led Snowball out to the mounting block, and a few moments later they were trotting away down the lane.

The lost cottage was not far enough away for her to need the pony—she could have got there almost as quickly on foot—but she loved being out on Snowball, and when she had fed Lady, the vixen, she and Peter, if he was there, could take the pony on as they often did, taking turns to ride him. And if there was no sign of Peter, then she would go down onto the levels for a canter by herself. And Snowball perfectly understood and approved of the plan, and stepped out, tossing his head and snuffing at the spring-time.

They took one of their special short cuts, down by the dike where the silver tufts of the goat willows were powdered gold with pollen, past the field where Caleb and Daisy and Dolly were at their harrowing, struck into the lane that led towards the village, and almost at once turned off into the old half-lost track through the woods. In the usual place she reined in and slithered from the saddle, hitched Snowball to the usual low-hanging branch, and disappeared with her bag of scraps into the mazy tangle of the woodland.

There was dog's mercury underfoot, and in an open place the first faintly scented wood-violets growing between the roots of an old tree. The buds were already coral-tipped on the branches of the squat wind-shaped oak trees. The sea was sounding today, even among the trees, though there was scarcely any wind. And Damaris, checking to listen, knew that the tide was on the turn, and knew also that there would

17

be wind again, and rain before nightfall.

It was just after she moved on again and was almost within sight of the cottage, that rounding a tangle of bramble and honeysuckle she almost fell over a man in rough seaman's clothes lying face down between the roots of an oak tree across her path.

Something seemed to check and then turn over itself inside her; she felt a scream rising in her throat and she wanted to turn and run, because it seemed very likely that he might be dead. But she managed to swallow the scream, and taking a deep and careful breath, knelt down beside him. His face was not quite hidden, for it was resting on his arm and turned a little to one side; and by putting her own face on the ground among the dog's mercury, she was able to get some kind of look at it.

It was young and bony and at the moment very white. A strand of dark hair pulled free from the queue at the back of his neck, fell forward across it, and as she looked, the dry rough end of it stirred to a small puff of breath from his half-open mouth.

With a little sound of relief that was almost a sob, she sat back and began to look for his hurt. It did not take long to find. In his left leg just below the knee where the thick seaman's stocking disappeared into his breeches was a dark soggy patch, almost black at the edges but still juicily red in the middle. Blood. And blood all down his leg and into his shoe and blood soaking into the ground beneath.

Damaris remembered last night's pistol shots.

He must have been lying out in the woods ever since, or just wandering until he dropped. He was not anyone she knew, so probably he was a stranger to these parts, one of the men who came from further off to help get the contraband cargoes away. But if he was a smuggler (he was certainly not a Customs House man) he looked like a sea smuggler more than

18

a land one. The one thing Damaris knew with absolute certainty was that whoever he was, whatever he was, she was on his side.

Better to leave his wound alone for the moment, the bleeding seemed to have nearly stopped. She began to pull up armfuls of last year's dead bracken and pile it over him, partly to keep him warm—he looked so cold, grey cold—partly to keep him hidden, from smugglers and Customs men alike; for until they knew more about him it might be better that no one but herself and Peter should know anything about him at all. She parted the brown fronds and took one more anxious look at his face, then kilted up her skirts and set off once more through the woods, not by the way she had come— Snowball must wait, she would be quicker and less noticeable without him—but by the shortest way to the village.

Somerley Green was shaped like a kind of long crescent, its cottages strung out along the curving lane, with the Big House and its farm buildings at one end, Genty the Wise Woman's cottage lost in the woods at the other, and the Church and the black-smith's and the wheelwright's and the Mermaid ale-house and the vicarage all clustered near the middle, round the Green that gave it its name.

It was not long before Damaris came to the edge of the trees and saw the warm russet straggle of the village before her, and a short while later, still panting from the speed she had made through the woods, she was crouching under the overgrown bushes of the vicarage garden. She could see the study window beyond which Peter would most like be at his Latin again under the stern eye of his father. But how to get hold of him and no questions asked was quite another matter.

Finally she cupped her hands round her mouth and

made the best imitation she could manage of the haunting woodwind call of an oyster-catcher, the private signal to Peter that she was there and wanted him. The Vicar was not really a countryman, and would not think it odd that an oyster-catcher should be heard so far from the tide-line, let alone in his shrubbery; but Peter, who had spent most of one afternoon teaching her the call, would know it well enough. She waited a few moments and then repeated the call, three times altogether. She did not dare to make it any more, lest somebody else who knew the habits of oyster-catchers—Ben who looked after the garden and the Vicar's fat cob, for instance—should overhear.

Behind the panes of the study window there was a flicker of movement that was not just the reflection of a flying bird, but for a while, nothing more. She waited while the time crawled by, hardly able to breathe in her impatience. Then somewhere at the far side of the house a door opened and shut. Another waiting time crept by, and then with only the faintest rustle among the bushes, suddenly Peter was beside her.

'That was the worst oyster-catcher I've ever heard,' he told her.

'You've taken your time! I thought you were never coming!' she whispered accusingly.

He gave a half breath of a laugh. 'It took a while to convince Father that he had promised to go and visit Silas Bundy this afternoon, and him laid by with the rheumatics. What is it, anyway?'

'I'll tell you on the way. Only come quick! I think he may die—'

But somehow she felt that already there was less chance of that happening, now that Peter was here. Peter with his square dependable face and thatch of mousey hair and rather serious gaze would somehow

20

not let it happen. He was that kind of person.

'Who may die?'

'My smuggler.'

They were working their way down the side of the garden by that time, and he checked among a mass of lilac suckers. 'You're gammoning me!'

'I'm *not*! I promise you I'm not. I found him quite close to Joyous Gard and he's been shot in the leg. Oh do come *on*!'

'Look,' said Peter after a moment, not coming on, 'all right, you're not gammoning: I believe you. Now you'd better go home and forget all about it. I'll find him and see what's to be done.'

Damaris snatched a breath of exasperation. 'Oh don't sound so grown up! You're only a year older than me. How could I possibly go home and forget about it? He's *my smuggler* and of course I'm coming back with you!'

She was already scrambling through the roots of the hedge, and the last words came muffled in leaf mould.

Peter said nothing more, and she heard him coming behind her. They gained the shelter of the ditch down the side of Glebe Field, and took to the woods.

Chapter 3: The Wise Woman

When they reached the place where Damaris had left her smuggler, the piled bracken had been flung aside, and the young man had heaved himself over onto an elbow and was peering about him in a dazed kind of way, with a pistol held rather shakily in his hand.

'Don't shoot,' Peter called breathlessly, 'were friends.'

And next instant Damaris was squatting beside him, saying in the voice she kept for young or injured things about the farm, 'Don't be afraid, we'll not hurt you.'

'Where—who—' began the young man muzzily, frowning up at her.

Peter came straight to essentials, 'Where's he shot?'

'In the leg like I told you. His left leg, just below the knee. —Oh be careful, Peter!'

The young man let out a kind of cracked breath of laughter, 'A pair of children!' And then, 'Do I gather—that we have met before?'

'Yes. At least, it was me that found you,' Damaris told him. 'Lie still, now.'

But she had no need to tell him that, for as Peter turned aside the bracken that still covered his legs and bent to peer at the red hole below his knee, the young man gave a gasp and lay back very still indeed, with his eyes shut and his lower lip caught between his teeth.

'He's been shot, all right,' Peter said after a moment. 'It's a bit of a mess.'

Damaris looked up from the young man's rigid face. 'What shall we do?'

Peter considered. 'It's none too warm out here,' he said at last. 'And I'd not be surprised if it was blowing up for rain—you can hear it in the tree-tops. We can't let him lie out in it. Best get him along to Tumbledown and safe under cover before we do anything else. You've got Snowball?'

'He's hitched in the usual place, I'll get him.'

When she got back, leading the fat white pony behind her—the underbrush and low-hanging branches were too dense for riding in that part of the woods—Peter had taken the young man's spotted neckerchief and tied it tightly over the bullet hole. 'He's not more than half with us,' he said, 'we'll just have to get him across Snowball's back some-how. . . .' He picked up the pistol which had fallen from the smuggler's hand. 'Empty.' He dropped it into his own pocket and stood up.

Damaris hitched the pony's bridle over a branch as close as she could get him alongside her smuggler, and set to work with Peter to get the young man to his feet.

'Now up with you—your arm round my neck,' Peter was saying. 'Steady.'

The pony snorted and sidled, misliking the smell of blood, and Damaris's smuggler, who as Peter had said, was only half with them anyway, had about as much strength in him as a shock of wet barley. But mercifully he was lightly built, and somehow, she never quite knew how, they got him across the saddle with his head and arms hanging down one side and his legs hanging down the other.

Then, with Damaris leading the pony, and Peter walking alongside to push back the low branches and keep the smuggler from sliding off one side or the other, they set off for Joyous Gard. It was only a stone's throw—if you could have thrown a stone in that dense undergrowth—a few seconds of bobbing flight for a woodpecker; but when the trees suddenly fell back and they came out into the tiny clearing screened only by goat willows and gorse bushes and a wild-duck skein of wind-shaped hawthorns from the rife and the open marsh beyond, and pulled up at the doorway of the ruined cottage, Damaris's smuggler slid off on top of Peter who tried to take his weight and then went over backwards under him. He had lost the kind of half-awakeness that he had had before, and the neckerchief was turning soggy red over the bullet hole.

But between them, Peter taking him under the shoulders and Damaris by the heels, though she was terrified of doing still more hurt to his wounded leg, they dragged him over the threshold and across to the far side of the one room, where the ragged thatch still clung to the rafters and at least there would be shelter from the coming rain.

At one side of the broken hearth, Lady sat upright

on her bracken bed, like a prick-eared shadow among the other shadows, watching them.

'Lady's food!' Damaris said, 'I dropped it when I found my smuggler—I'll be back,' and she fled.

She was gone only a couple of minutes, but when she got back Peter was already carrying in armfuls of bracken and piling them into another bed. 'I've shortened Lady's chain,' he said, 'so that she can't get over to the other corner just for a while.'

Damaris nodded, and emptied the bag of scraps in front of the little vixen. She hated to see how short the chain attached to the old dog-collar round her neck now was, but she quite saw that Lady must be kept close in her own corner for a while. She longed to stay and explain to her, and feed her scrap by scrap as she usually did; but today there were other things to be done first, and she left her to snap up the cheese rinds and crusts and bits of bacon in front of her, and went to help Peter with the bracken bed in the other corner.

They got the young man onto it bit by bit, while Lady, having finished her food, sat in her own corner and watched them still. Then they undid the necker-chief, and Peter got out his pocket-knife and slit the blood-stiffened breeks to above his knee and rolled the stocking down, and side by side they took a long careful look at the bullet hole. The man was still unconscious, which was maybe as well for him.

The bleeding had almost stopped again, but look-ing at her smuggler's face under its ragged forelock of dark hair, Damaris had a frightened feeling that that might be because there was no more blood inside him to come out. She pushed the forelock back, and wondered rather desperately what they should do next.

Meanwhile Peter was examining the wound more closely. He had once helped to get a gamekeeper's bullet out of one of the local poachers, and knew about such things; knew at any rate that a bullet that had passed through left two holes, the one where it had gone in, and a bigger and more ragged one where it had come out. Here, there was only the one.

He looked up. 'The bullet's still there.'

Damaris sat back on her heels and stared at him. 'Can you get it out?'

He shook his head. 'I daren't. It's lodged somehow.'

'Who then? Doctor Godwyn?'

'Take a long time to get him, all the way from Chichester. Besides . . .'

Besides, neither of them knew how Doctor Godwyn might feel about smugglers and handing them over to the authorities.

'There's Matthew Binns up at the Big House,' Peter said slowly; and again there was silence. Matthew Binns the Farringtons' head groom was certainly the best horse-doctor for miles around, and not much doubt that he was deep in with the smugglers, the Fair Traders, but there was something dark and slantwise about him, and . . . 'I don't know,' Damaris said. 'He's not from round these parts, or we'd have seen him before. He might be from a rival gang or something.'

She had heard ugly stories of what could happen between gangs.

And then the answer came to her, 'There's Genty Small.'

Genty Small the Wise Woman, who seemed to live half in the same world as other people and half in a world of her own—'Cracked in the cock-loft,' Peter had said of her before now—and who would not care if the young man was a smuggler nor what gang he came from, so long as he was hurt and needed her skill.

'Do you suppose she'll be able to get a bullet out?' Peter asked, doubtfully.

'I'll go and ask her. At any rate she'll know who can, and meanwhile she'll be able to help him with her herbs and simples. I'll go now. You stay here with him and get a fire going and some water on to heat—she's bound to want hot water—Oh and Lady'll want some water, too.'

'I'd not be surprised if I hadn't watered Lady just as often as you have,' Peter said peaceably, 'you'd best tear me the hem off your petticoat before you go; I'll need something more than this sopping neckerchief to bind up his leg.'

Damaris gathered up her skirts and untied the draw-strings at her waist, and the white cotton petticoat fell at her feet. 'You can have it all,' she said, stepping out of it. 'It's a very old one. I can always tell Aunt Selina we tore it up for polishing rags last autumn and doesn't she remember.'

And she whisked out through the nettle-grown doorway.

All the way to Genty's cottage she was wild with anxiety lest the Wise Woman should be out somewhere, gathering simples or the like. But when she came out into the wood-shore clearing just short of the village, Genty in a sacking apron was on her knees busy among the herbs in her garden, with her white nanny-goat tethered close by, while her little smoke-grey cat Grizelda sat in the middle of the grass path, watching her.

Damaris hesitated a moment. She knew Genty quite well: Aunt Selina always bought honeycomb from her to make her own renowned herb posset with which she dosed the household when they had colds; and Madge from the dairy went to her for green ointment for her chilblains and more than once for a charm posy to wear in church to help her catch

27

the eye of whichever of the village lads she was interested in at the moment; but even so, she was a little shy of going alone to the cottage on the edge of the woods.

But as she paused at the gap in the sweetbriar hedge—Genty had no gate to her garden—the old woman got slowly to her feet and turned towards her; a brown-skinned old woman, tough and twisted as a tree root, with eyes that must have been the brightest blue when she was young, and a mass of hair that should have been grey but was still as black and glossy as a rook's wing, bundled up under a man's weather-faded stocking cap.

'Good-day to 'ee, liddle mistress, would it be something for your Auntie, then?'

Damaris shook her head, getting her breath back, and as soon as she could, began to tell the Wise Woman about her smuggler—if of course he was a smuggler.

Before she had finished, she found herself inside the small dark cottage, for slow and gentle though she was in all her movements, Genty was not one to waste time when there was no time to waste. 'And the bullet is still there,' she was saying. 'At least Peter thinks it is. And we're not sure about Doctor Godwyn—not if he's a smuggler; and Matthew Binns up at the Big House . . .'

'You might be right not to trust that one. You might be right to come to ol' Genty, aye, sure-lye.' She was moving about, taking things from a cupboard in the corner and putting them into an osier basket that she had set on the table. 'He'll have lost a deal of blood, I daresay, aye, and like enough still losing it? Well here's the means to help that; and fever-few seethed in milk—that's a sovereign remedy against the wound-fever.' She reached up and chose this and that from among the bunches of dried herbs and roots hanging from the smoke-blackened rafters. 'Comfrey's God's own gift for the healing of a wound, specially if there's a bone needs mending too—and yarrow that the good folk in churches call the Devil's own. . . .'

The little grey cat stalked over to sit on the bright rag rug before the fire, and Damaris stood in the middle of the narrow, crowded, firelit, many-shadowed room, and looked about her as her eyes grew more used to the shadows; seeing the pots and jars and dried bundles that crowded the wall shelves and hung from the ceiling and stood on the window-ledge and left scarcely room for moving; and smelling the odd mingled smells of the place, and wishing that Genty would not take so long to consider each of the things she put in her basket.

But in a surprisingly short time, even so, the basket was almost ready, and Genty was opening an old carved chest that stood under the window. Craning to see what was in it, Damaris could only glimpse more bundles and a beautiful small case of painted leather with clasps that shone like gold. 'This is where I keep all my wicked things,' the Wise Woman said, unlocking it, and brought out from it something quite small, long and narrow and wrapped in fine white linen. She re-locked the case—the only locked thing, it seemed, in all the cottage—and stowed the key back somewhere inside her clothes; then, straightening up, turned back the linen folds. The window light slipped along the blade of a slim vicious-looking knife and a couple of other brightly polished tools the like of which Damaris had never seen before.

'A barber-surgeon I once did a good turn to gave me these and showed me how to use them when he was too old to use them himself any more.' Genty shook her head over them. 'I've no liking for the Cold

Iron; but if the bullet be still there—aye well, there's things that the Cold Iron has its uses for.' She tucked the linen-wrapped bundle down the side of the basket, and turned back to the cupboard. 'Clean rags for bandages.'

'I've left my petticoat there,' Damaris told her. 'It's quite clean.'

'Can't have too many—they'll be needed another day,' said Genty, and added them to the basket. 'Lights now, my dearie. The day will be fading soon, and we shall need light to work by.'

'We've got an old lantern, but we're short on candles to go in it.'

Genty rummaged in another corner, and added a handful of tallow dips. From somewhere beyond a low inner door she brought a pipkin of goat's milk; she laid turfs over the fire, and disappearing up a steep ladder-stairway that must lead to her sleeping place, she came back with a rough brown blanket smelling of rosemary.

'You take that,' she said to Damaris, 'an' the milk, an' don't 'ee spill it. And to the little grey cat, 'Now my lover, mind an' guard the house an' keep all happy till I come back.'

Then she went out, shooing Damaris ahead of her and leaving the cottage door wide open behind.

Chapter 4: Skills and Remedies

By the time they got back to Joyous Gard the light was going fast. Snowball was fading from a solid pony to a pale shadow in the dusk, and the first fine mizzle rain was spitting down the wind that had begun to rise.

Peter had got a fire going on the broken hearth, and filled both their water pots and a chipped cup with water, and the biggest pot, propped over the fire, was coming up to the bubble. The eyes of the little vixen lying nose-on-paws in her own corner caught the flamelight and shone unwinking like two green elf-lamps in the gloom. In the other corner, the young man lying under their moth-eaten horse rug, was awake again, and his face turned anxiously towards the doorway and the dusk beyond, though he made no move to reach for the empty pistol which lay beside him. He relaxed with a small sigh when he saw that the comers were only Damaris and a little old woman carrying a basket.

'You again,' he said.

Genty dumped the basket and knelt down at his side. 'Been playing hare-and-hounds with the Customs men, have 'ee?' she said. Then as he made no reply, 'Aye well, no questions asked and none to answer. Now let old Genty take a look—but first a listen, my dearie.'

And she pulled his jacket and shirt open and bent to press her ear to his chest. As she did so, they all saw the oilskin-covered packet that hung on a grubby white ribbon around his neck. He made a quick fumbling movement to hide it from their eyes. Genty put her own tree-root hand over his, and moved both it and the packet aside. 'Whatever you have there is no concern of ours,' she said. ''Tis just your heart I would be listenin' to . . . An' 'tis a good strong one that ye have plodding away there under your ribs.' She sat back, drawing his shirt together again. 'Light the liddle ol' lantern, boy, and we'll take a look at this knee.'

She turned the rug aside, and gave her attention to the bullet hole below his left knee, while Peter got the lantern lit and held it close. 'Aye, 'tis still there—and the sooner 'tis out the better,' she said after a few moments.

The young man drew a small harsh breath. 'Who?—You?—'

'Aye, me,' said Genty. ''Twouldn't be the first time, an' like enough it won't be the last. Now, we'll need hot water—that's for you to see to, liddle mistress.'

'We've only got the two pots,' Damaris said

32

anxiously. 'One's nearly boiling, and the other's standing by. Shall I put that one on the fire as well?'

'Aye, do that. 'Twill serve for a start, and we can get some more from the spring later if need be.' Genty was busy among the contents of her basket. She had brought out the slim white bundle containing her surgeon's tools and laid them on the flat log that served in Joyous Gard as a table; now she brought out dried leaves and roots and gave them to Damaris. 'Now Lover, put these leaves in the boiling pot, that's just for bathing the wound after. Take it off the fire and set it aside when I tell you. Put the rest in the smaller pot, bring it up to the boil and keep it boiling—gently, mind, gently as a sleeping pigeon. Feed the fire liddle by liddle, so's the heat stays steady. An' whatever ye do, whatever ye hear, don't 'ee stop stirring the liddle pot with this—'tis a sprig of rowan wood—nor don't 'ee take your eye from it to look round.'

Damaris did as she was bidden. Behind her she heard Genty telling Peter how to fix the lantern so that the light fell where she wanted it; and then how to steady the smuggler's knee. 'Keep it turned out a liddle, your hand under it—so—now hold steady. . . .' And after that there was a time when she was only too glad to keep her mind on her boiling pots and think as little as might be about what was going on behind her.

She listened to the fine rain hushing across the roof and the spatter of it coming in where there was no roof to keep it out; and the rustling of the fire and the soft bubble of the boiling pots, and smelled the pungent steam that rose from them, making her eyes water. But she could not keep herself from hearing Genty's voice saying, 'Now—further this way—ah-ha—Do 'ee bear with it a while longer—' and the harsh gasping breath of her smuggler under the Wise

Woman's probing, any more than she could keep herself from smelling the dark slaughter-house smell of blood. The vixen whimpered, made uneasy by the smell. Damaris fed the fire little twigs and bits of bark from the pile beside it, and stirred the brew with her rowan twig, and tried not to shiver and feel sick. In a little there was a sharp gasp behind her, almost a cry cut off short, and then a long sigh, and Genty's voice: 'Tch, tch! He's off on his travels again. Well, 'twill be better for him so, till this be safe out.'

And then there was just the rain and the soft sea wind in the trees again for a while, and then Genty calling to her to take the bigger pot from the fire and set it aside to cool. A few moments later the Wise Woman said crooningly, 'Ah now, there ye are, ye liddle varmint—come to ol' Genty . . . co-ome . . . co-ome . . . There, 'tis out an' all's over.'

Damaris let her own breath go as though she had been holding it all the while.

And after that everything seemed to go suddenly quick and easy.

Genty bathed the wound and covered it with a kind of poultice of the leaves that Damaris had been boiling, and tightly bound it with strips from her old petticoat; and Peter and Genty between them eased the young man out of his jacket and rolled it up to make him a pillow, and Genty shook out the rough brown blanket and added it to the horse rug, pulling them both warmly to his chin. The scent of rosemary stole out from it to lighten the darker smells that had gathered in Joyous Gard.

Then she took half the milk which had been warming beside the fire, and poured it into a pottery cup which she had brought with her, and added some of the liquid from the smaller pot; lastly she took a small leather flask from her basket, worked out the wooden stopper and poured in a few drops of some thick amber-coloured fluid. A faint sleepy smell was added to all the other smells in the place. And as she slipped an arm under the young man's head to raise him, Damaris saw that her smuggler was halfway back inside himself again.

'Drink this. 'Tis sleep you need now, Lover.'

The young man's eyes were open but hazy, searching their faces with a frown of bewilderment. 'Come now, do 'ee drink, there's no harm in it, only sleep; an' sleep be what you need, aye, sure-lye.' Genty tipped the rim of the cup against his teeth, and he gulped down the warm brew, without, Damaris thought, really knowing that he did so.

She looked across at Peter; and he looked back at her and swallowed. There was blood on his hands that he was rubbing at with a spare bit of rag, and she thought he seemed a bit greenish in the upward light of the lantern.

Genty laid the young man down and again pulled the rugs to his chin, tucking his empty pistol in beside him like someone tucking in a child's toy. Then she beckoned Peter to bring the lantern over to the other corner, where Lady lay watching all that went forward, her eyes unwinking, her white-tipped brush wreathed across her muzzle, her injured paw thrust a little awkwardly out from her side.

'So here's another wounded one,' said Genty. 'Oh the ways of men an' their traps. . . . But this one be nigh on mended. Give her a few more days, an' then ye must let her go; 'tisn't good for the creatures of the wild to bide too long with humankind, lest they lose the way back to their own world after all.'

Damaris nodded. Something ached in her at the thought of the vixen going but she understood what must happen almost as well as Genty. 'Just a few more days, to be sure that her paw is quite healed and she can hunt for herself again. Then we meant to take her collar off and leave the door open.'

Genty said something softly to the vixen in a strange tongue—Damaris thought it was probably Romany—and Lady raised her head and made a small sound of her own in response.

'Love is never lost,' said the Wise Woman, seemingly to no one in particular. She straightened up and looked once again at the wounded smuggler. 'Sleeping like a lamb. Works quick, does ol' Genty's potion.'

'Will he be all right?' asked Peter, speaking almost for the first time.

'Aye, but I'll stay wi' him through the night, just to make certain-sure.'

Damaris looked at the young man's sleeping face. It still seemed so grey and hollowed-out. 'You promise?' she said. 'He—he won't die?'

Peter began, 'Now look, Genty *said* he'd be all right—'

But Genty also was gazing down into the young man's face that looked somehow open and unshielded in his sleep. One hand fumbled up under the blankets to find the oilskin packet about his neck. 'Aye, quite sure,' she said, 'when his time comes, 'twill not be here in his own land, but somewhere far off across the water. The Wildgoose mark of the Wanderer is on his forehead, an' there'll be no homecoming for him at the day's end.'

'I'll come with you,' Peter said, when Damaris had unhitched the wet and patiently waiting Snowball, just as though she had not made her own way home from Joyous Gard often enough before now. Well maybe not so late into the dusk of such a wild night; and she was not sorry to have him trudging along beside her.

The ruffled water of the rife gleamed mealy pale through the trees as she glanced back once to the gleam of lantern light in the cottage window; and the last rooks were flapping home, loud-voiced against the wind, to their roost in the vicarage elms.

At the edge of Dinder Meadow, with the candle-light of Carthagena shining out across the fallow, Peter checked. 'I'd best be getting back now—see you tomorrow, maybe?'

They looked at each other in the last-deepening of the dusk, not speaking of what had happened. Maybe it was the kind of thing best not talked about, away from Joyous Gard. Then he disappeared back into the trees, heading the same way as the rooks, and Damaris rode on along the field dike and into the lane.

Candlelight was streaming through the open door-way of the house, and there was a lantern bobbing in the steading yard in a golden halo of drifting rain; and just as she rode up to it, her father came out through the gateway, with Caleb and a couple of the farm-hands behind him.

'Here she is,' he called back to Aunt Selina who was hovering in the house doorway, and then he turned his attention to Damaris. 'Where in Heaven's name have you been, Dimmy?' (he was the only person who called her Dimmy, and he did it even when he was angry.) 'Have you any idea what o'clock it is? We were just coming to hunt for you.'

He lifted her down from Snowball's back, none too gently. 'All right, Caleb, take the pony. Now as for you, Miss—'

'Not out there in the rain, John,' Aunt Selina protested from the doorway. 'Surely to goodness it can wait till we have the child indoors?'

And Damaris found herself being run up the garden path and through the candlelit doorway, with her father's hand clamped uncomfortably tight on her arm. She had known that there would be explanations to be made when she got home, and had wondered if she could say that she had been with old Mrs Farrington. That had happened more than once, but always by invitation, and Aunt Selina would only have to mention it to Mrs Farrington for the whole story to fall apart. But by the time she was confronted by her family in the parlour, she had come by a better story to tell. 'I was with old Genty,' she told them. That much was true, anyway. 'My tooth started to ache again, and I was near her cottage, so I went in to ask her for something to make it stop; and she was there making a cordial for Granny Mason's chest, and she let me stop to watch. It takes a long time to make, that cordial, and I did not notice how late it was getting. And I'm sorry, Father. Sorry, Aunt Selina.'

She knew that Genty would not betray her or her smuggler; but she did hope Peter wasn't telling some story that would contradict hers. They should have thought that out on the way home. Then she decided that Peter would be most unlikely to be having to tell any story at all. Apart from the Latin lessons, his family were used to him coming and going at all hours.

Father seemed about to say something very terrible, while Aunt Selina hovered and clucked in the background. His eyes got worried and he breathed loudly through his nose, but he was never very good at dealing with his daughter; he might have been better with sons. In the end all he said was, 'Selina, this is for you to deal with. Do what you think proper.' And he strode off to his counting-house.

'You're a bad girl, and I should give you a sharp scold!' said Aunt Selina, doing her best. 'Such a bad girl, frightening us all like that! One cannot expect Genty—Oh dear, such a good creature, but not quite—I daresay she never thought to feed you—'

Damaris thought quickly, and decided that a lie was the honourable thing. 'Oh yes she did, Aunt Selina, we had bread and cheese and a sort of herb soup, and' (if you were going to lie, you might as well do it properly) 'and elderberry conserve.' And then, for she was human and hungry after all, 'but it *was* quite a long time ago.'

'There's some cold roast beef left from supper,' said Aunt Selina, 'and raisin tartlets. Go and get washed and comb your hair, child; oh dear, I can't conceive what your mother would have said: you really do look as though you had been pulled through a furze-bush backwards!'

Chapter 5: Tom Wildgoose

Next morning Damaris woke before anyone else was astir—except of course Caleb and Dick in the stables, and Sim Bundy in the lambing fold who had probably never been to bed—and as soon as she had huddled some clothes on, she slipped down stairs and got busy in the larder and dairy. She was used to gathering scraps for Lady, but this was a more serious matter. It would have been easy enough if she could simply have cut a large wedge of cheese and another of game pie and taken a loaf from yesterday's baking. But Hannah the old maid would certainly notice that, so she finished up by taking just a little of everything in sight, and bundling it all in a clean pudding-cloth, cold beef and raised pie and stale bread and cheese and a raisin tartlet all together. Then she filled a stoneware bottle with milk—like enough ale would be more welcome, but milk would be more suitable for someone with a bullet hole in him—and stowed the lot together with Lady's scraps in her own egg-basket, slipped out by the kitchen door and hid it at the back of the brushwood pile. That safely done, she came in, carefully putting the bar up again and behind her, and creeping upstairs, was back in her own room in time to get up when the rest of the household did.

The very first moment she could escape from Selina and her lessons, she was away, with the precious basket retrieved from its hiding place, safe under her cloak, heading back for Joyous Gard.

The rain had passed in the night, and there were wet gleams of sunshine lancing through the woods, and the birds singing in the tone of freshly washed surprise that belongs to the first days of springtime. And when she reached the ruined cottage, the door, what remained of it, was propped half-open, and Lady, her chain loosed to full length again, lay along the threshold, nose-on-paws in the thin sunshine.

Damaris knelt down beside the little vixen and began to feed her, fondling her dark-tipped ears and beautiful bracken-red neck the while, and talking to her very softly. 'Soon now, but not just yet, just a few days more, till your paw is quite well again.' And when the last scrap was gone, she gave her a parting touch under her creamy chin, and getting up slipped past her into the shadows of the ruined cottage beyond.

Genty must have long since gone off about her own affairs, and the smuggler was awake, and had heard her outside with Lady, for he was up on one elbow, his faced turned to the doorway as she came in. He was still very white, but he seemed to be properly back inside himself again, and greeted her with a somewhat crooked smile. 'So here's two of us on your hands to be looked after. I feel myself scarce in a fit state to be receiving ladies.'

'You look to be much better than you were last night,' Damaris told him. 'I've brought you some food. Do you think you can eat?'

He hitched himself higher onto his elbow to look down into the folds of the pudding-cloth she was by that time untying, and winced as the movement clawed at his wounded knee.

She checked in her task. 'Oh your poor leg, is it hurting very badly?'

'Not so badly as it was,' he said quickly. 'Little Mistress, may I put this aside for a while? Your brother was here earlier, and I am well filled with bread and cheese.'

'My brother? Oh you mean Peter.' Damaris put the bundle on the flat log. 'He's not my brother, he's Peter Ballard from the vicarage.'

'And you?' said Damaris's smuggler.

'I'm Damaris Crocker from Carthagena Farm.' She smiled at him, glad that they were getting to an exchange of names. 'This is our secret place.' She hesitated a moment, afraid that he would laugh at her. 'I call it Joyous Gard, after Sir Lancelot's castle in the *Morte d'Arthur*. *You* know.'

A smile flickered into the young man's eyes. '*I* know.'

'But Peter says that's too flowery. He just calls it Tumbledown.'

'Peter has no imagination,' said the young man. Then he grew serious. 'And you found me and got me here to your secret place.'

'It's not far, and we had my pony.'

He frowned. 'I can just remember—in a kind of fog. It seems I have to thank the two of you for my life. . . . You and the old woman who was here. . . .'

42

'That's Genty the Wise Woman. The bullet was still in your leg and we had to find someone to get it out. We didn't dare risk the doctor because we don't know how he feels about smugglers.'

The young man's brows flicked up. 'And you know how Genty the Wise Woman feels about smugglers?'

'She doesn't—I mean—she only feels about people. People and animals and the woods.'

There was a little silence; only Lady's chain chimed faintly as she moved, and the light fluttered as the wind stirred the willow branches beyond the great hole in the thatch, and somewhere along the rife the sandpipers were calling. After the silence had lasted a while, Damaris said, 'Now I have told you all our names, but I do not know yours.' And then as still he did not answer, she added, 'But maybe you don't want to tell?'

'I crave your pardon,' said the young man, 'that was very discourteous of me. My name is Tom: Tom—Wildgoose.'

Damaris saw and heard the tiny hesitation, and remembered Genty's words last night. 'The Wild-goose mark of the Wanderer is on his forehead,' the Wise Woman had said. Maybe he had not been as deep asleep as he seemed, or the words had reached down to him where he was, however deep. They looked at each other, the young man not asking to be believed, Damaris not believing, but knowing that she must not ask beyond the name he chose to give.

'Tom Wildgoose,' she said, and then, 'Are you a sea-smuggler?'

'Why should I be?'

'I don't know. Peter and I thought you looked more like a sea-smuggler than the land kind.'

'I am flattered,' said Tom Wildgoose. 'The seamen always consider themselves the aristocrats of the trade—but the fact is that I am not a smuggler at all.'

'Not a Customs House man? We thought it was one of them that shot you.'

'It was. But I'm not a smuggler for all that. I was, as one might say, part of the cargo. The Fair Traders carry other things than brandy and lace.'

'What things?' Damaris asked.

He did not answer at once; and when he did, his voice was becoming woolly at the edges as though with sleep. 'Oh—spies, secret letters—news that never appears in the news sheets nor the Gentlemen's Magazine.'

She waited for more, playing with a dry brown frond pulled from the bedding bracken; but no more came, and when she looked up he was lying with his face turned away from her into the shadows. Well, sleep was probably the thing he needed just now, more than anything else, even food or someone to talk to. She sat quiet beside him for a little while. Then she got up, and stowed the food and milk in the square wall recess that had maybe once been a cupboard, well above his head where Lady would not be able to reach it, and pulled up the rugs that he had thrust down, seeing as she did so that his hand had gone back into the breast of his shirt and was closed over the oilskin packet on its grubby white ribbon.

Lady was standing in the doorway on all four paws, as Damaris checked to stroke her head in going out. Tomorrow might be the time to let her go. Meanwhile she would be company for Tom Wild-goose.

Damaris was in time for midday dinner in the big kitchen, which was just as well, for her father was not in the best of tempers. Young Mr Farrington from the Big House and some of his fine London guests that he was for ever having down to stay with him, had been out riding, and crossing the seaward-stretching tongue of Carthagena land had left a gate open so that some of the bullocks had got into the winter wheat. It was not the first time that it had happened.

'Maybe you should be thankful they used the gate, John dear,' said Aunt Selina, trying to soothe him down. 'It is not as though they had broken through the hedge.'

''Twouldn't have been the first time, if they had,' growled one of the farmhands into his pease pudding. (All the farm ate together in the kitchen at midday, according to the old custom, except of course for the horsemen, who did not eat until the horses had been brought in from work a couple of hours later.)

John Crocker was not to be soothed. 'Him and his fine London cronies. You'd think none of them had ever seen a field or a field gate before!'

'They're young,' said Aunt Selina, 'just young and thoughtless.'

'Old Mr Farrington was young once, but I don't remember that he ever left gates open. He was a proper countryman, of course—knew about the working of a farm instead of leaving it all to his bailiff as his fine gentleman son does!'

John Crocker snorted, and began to carve slices off the mutton as though he was carving them off young Mr Farrington.

It was afternoon before Damaris managed to get away, the day after that, and just short of Joyous Gard she met Peter bound in the same direction. Genty was already there and pouring some sharp-smelling herb brew down Tom Wildgoose. The young man was flushed and restless, with eyes that looked too bright and too far sunk into his head.

'Oh!' Damaris ran in, forgetting even to greet Lady, and squatted down beside him, 'Oh, he's worse!'

''Tis the wound fever,' Genty said. ''Twas a'most bound to come upon him. Now that you're here, I'll be off back to my own place, for there's things I need. Do 'ee bide here while I'm away; I'll not be long.'

'Tell us what we're to do while you're gone, Genty,' Damaris said.

'Naught to do. 'Tis just that there should be someone here. Do the two of 'ee just sit outside where ye can hear him if he rouses, and give him a drink from the pipkin if he asks for it. But he'll not rouse, wi' the draught I've given him, and he'll be best left to himself.'

So in a little, when the Wise Woman was gone, they settled themselves before the sagging doorway in the March sunshine. Lady, full of household scraps, lay nose-on-paws between them.

They did not talk much for fear of disturbing the wounded man sleeping restlessly in the shadows behind them. Damaris had already told Peter what little she had learned of Tom Wildgoose the day before, and anyhow, they were comfortably used to being silent in each other's company, especially in the woods. But after a while Damaris asked at half breath, 'If he's not a smuggler, what do you suppose he is?'

Peter shook his head. 'I don't know,' he said slowly. 'He could be a spy.'

Damaris felt a small sudden chill inside herself. 'That packet round his neck? Oh Peter—no—'

Peter was fondling Lady behind the ears, and his hand checked in the caressing movement until she muzzle-tipped his hand for more. 'I don't know,' he said again, soberly, 'but I suppose we ought to try and find out.'

'No!' Damaris protested, 'I *don't* suppose we ought to try and find out! Anyway we're not at war with France, now!'

'No, but we mostly are,' Peter said. 'They could be getting ready for the next time.' Suddenly he turned and saw her anxious face. 'Little goose! Let's forget about it. There's nothing we could do this afternoon, anyhow.'

And the silence settled between them again. But in a little while something happened that pushed the question of whether or not Tom Wildgoose was a spy into the backs of their minds for the time being.

Peter said very softly, 'Look—over there beyond the big thorn tree.' And following the direction of his eyes, Damaris saw a flicker of red-brown movement in the undergrowth. And as she held her breath, a few moments later, out from the tangle of furze and bramble and hawthorn trotted a big dog fox. Just for an instant he checked, muzzle raised to smell the wind, and the sunlight kindled his coat to the brilliant hot-coal colour that had always seemed to her to be the colour of joy itself.

Only a moment the magic lasted, then he doubled back into the mazy bramble thicket, and was gone. 'Oh-h!' she whispered, 'Oh he was beautiful!'

Lady did not seem to have seen him, and still lay contentedly between them, nose on paws. But a minute or so later Damaris felt a kind of faint thrill running through the vixen; and at the same instant, Peter took his fondling hand away. 'He must be up-wind of us, and she's getting his scent.'

Lady came to her feet, and stood with up-raised muzzle in her turn, sniffing the wind, her head turned in the direction where the dog fox must be.

And Damaris knew that the time had come for her

to go back to the wild. Peter too. He said, 'Will you do it, or shall I?'

'You,' Damaris said. She stroked the smooth red head between the dark-tipped ears for the last time, in farewell.

There was an aching in her throat as she watched Peter's hands on the buckle of the old dog-collar, slipping it free, rubbing the place where the collar had been. 'Go then. Free now.'

The vixen looked up into Damaris's face. 'Goodbye, Lady. Don't quite forget us,' Damaris said. But Lady was already trotting off. In a few moments she too had disappeared into the undergrowth.

'She didn't even look back,' Damaris said.

There was the faintest frowing among the bushes, and Genty Small stepped out into the clearing, with a filled basket on her arm, and the white nanny-goat on the end of its tether in her hand. 'She wouldn',' said the Wise Woman. 'She's away to her own kind; but she'll not forget 'ee for all that.'

'A dog fox came by and she got his scent,' Peter was loosing the old dog-collar from the chain. 'Do you suppose he was her mate?'

'A' might be, though 'tis like a' would have taken more interest in this place. She's a young vixen. Sometimes they don't think about mating so early in the first spring.' She stood looking after Lady for a moment, the basket propped on her hip, while the nanny began to lip at the rough grass. Then she glanced in through the sagging doorway. 'He didn't waken? Aye, that's well; 'tis sleep a' needs more than all else; sleep and ol' Genty's fever draught, an' milk—I'll tether Maudlin and she'll see to that. . . . Now do 'ee be gettin' off home, my lovers.'

'There's nothing we can do to help?' Peter asked.

'Later; aye, sure-lye. But now tes just for me and my skills. God an' the Good Folk go with 'ee.'

So they knew they were dismissed.

'I'll come back with you,' Peter said. 'Will Aunt Selina give me some supper, do you suppose? I promised Sim Bundy I'd give him a hand in the lambing fold tonight.'

Chapter 6: The Oilskin Packet

For two days the fever lasted, and Genty remained at Joyous Gard, scarcely letting Damaris or Peter through the door, which Damaris felt was hard. Tom Wildgoose, smuggler or spy or no, was hers. She was happy to share him with Peter, as she shared most things. But it was rather different to have a third person, even Genty, there and not sharing him at all. But she had enough sense to keep all that to herself; and ran the Wise Woman's errands, to fetch things from her cottage, and put down food for Grizelda without any protest.

Peter seemed not to mind so much, and whenever he could get away from Latin with his father, there was always the busy lambing fold for him to turn to. ('You did ought to be a shepherd: proper way wi' the ewes ye've got,' Sim Bundy told him, and Peter flushed with pleasure at the old shepherd's praise.)

But on the third morning, when Damaris arrived at Joyous Gard, the nanny-goat was no longer picketed in the little clearing, and when she slipped in through the half-open doorway there was no sign of the Wise Woman, and Tom Wildgoose was lying propped high on a thick roll of dry bracken, looking more like a real person and less like the flushed and restless shell of one.

'You're better!' Damaris said.

'I'm better,' Tom Wildgoose agreed, 'much more the thing.' He managed a rather crooked smile. 'I'm being a most unconscionable nuisance to all of you.'

'You're not!' Damaris said indignantly, squatting down beside him, her bundle in her lap. 'You're—' she hesitated, seeking the right word, and came out with one that was a favourite with Aunt Selina, 'I think you're very *romantic*!'

He gave a weak croak of laughter. 'I don't *feel* romantic, I feel like a half-drowned kitten, which is confounded awkward, because the sooner I'm away from here the better.'

'Not yet,' Damaris said quickly, 'you'll be stronger soon, and you mustn't go until you are . . . Besides—'

'Besides?'

'Oh I don't know. I hate people going away. First Lady—'

'The little vixen? You did not let her go because of me? Having to feed me as well? Something like that?'

'No. Her paw was mended, and Genty said it was time to let her go.'

'And Genty, I am sure would be right. But I don't think she is quite gone yet. I saw her in the doorway

51

last night, just at twilight. I don't believe I dreamed her.'

'Oh, I wish I'd been here! Do you think she will come again?'

'I should think very likely—for a while. This is a good refuging place; when I go away from here, I think I would come back if I could.' He had spoken the last bit very softly. Then he added in quite a different tone, 'Damaris, would there be something to eat in that bundle? Genty gave me bread and milk before she went, but that was quite a long time ago.'

Damaris hesitated. 'Yes, I did bring some bits, just in case—But Genty didn't say anything about not having any more to eat because of the fever, or—or anything of that sort, did she?'

'No, she didn't; I promise you she didn't, on my honour, Mistress Damaris.'

'I'll trust you,' Damaris decided, untying the knots of her little bundle. 'There's some raised pie and some gingerbread and the heel of a loaf. The rest is just scraps, like—like I used to bring for Lady.'

Tom eyed the food hungrily.

'If there's more than you can eat—' Damaris began, and hesitated.

'There isn't. But there's more than Genty would approve of my eating. Do you think Lady might feel like the scraps, if she comes again?'

He pulled himself further up on his bed of piled bracken, shaking his head as though to clear it, and leaned forward to take the small ragged lump of pie she held out to him; and as he did so the breast of his tattered shirt fell open, and she saw that the oilskin packet on its ribbon was gone from round his neck.

As though he felt her questioning gaze, he glanced up quickly, and saw where she was looking, and smiled. 'Only some papers that—had best not be found on me if I should be taken. They're in a safe place,' he jerked a thumb towards the doorway.

'But you can't walk yet,' Damaris said.

'I didn't walk. I did a fine imitation of a caterpillar. Slow and not very elegant, but I had plenty of time once Genty was gone. And the undergrowth is thick and the earth soft round Joyous Gard.'

Then Damaris said a stupid thing. She knew it was stupid the moment she had said it; but she had not meant to say it at all.

'You're not a spy, are you? Oh please, you're not a spy?'

He looked at her in silence for a long breath of time. Then he said 'I could be, of course, could I not?'

'No!' she said quickly. 'Anyway England and France aren't at war now.'

'But they generally are. And like enough we soon shall be again.'

'That's what Peter said.'

'Sensible Peter. Does he think that of me, then?'

'No. He just—isn't sure. . . .'

'But you are, well, almost sure?' The strange young man put down his lump of pie, and took her chin between a crumby finger and thumb, and tipped it up to look into her face. 'There are letters in that packet which like most letters, should not be read by anyone save the people they are meant for. But there is nothing in them that can harm England or make a featherweight of difference to fat King George on his throne.' There was a kind of mockery in his tone, but as though it was himself he mocked at; and a bitter brightness in his eyes that was nothing to do with the fever that had so lately left him, and which she did not understand. 'I promise you I'm not a spy.'

Damaris had not known that she was holding her breath, until she let it go in a long sigh. 'Of course you're not a spy,' she said. 'Now eat up your gingerbread, and I'll put the scraps out for Lady.'

And she wondered why he laughed.

Over the next few days Damaris and Peter between them kept Tom Wildgoose in food and company, coming and going as chance offered; sometimes one, sometimes the other, sometimes both together; sometimes finding him alone, sometimes finding Genty with him and the place reeking of her wound-salves and herbal remedies. Twice, Lady appeared, like a russet shadow, coming half back from the wild to eat the scraps put out for her, though she did not come even as far as the doorway, and Damaris felt that as long as she came at all, they still made a kind of unbroken circle. Peter said no more as to his suspicions that the wounded man might be a spy; indeed it was Peter who on the second day produced a well-worn translation of *Don Quixote*, saying 'Thought you might like something to read; it must be devilish dull here when none of us are by.'

Tom Wildgoose took it and looked with pleasure at the title page, 'An old friend to keep me company. But will your father not miss it?'

'It's not out of Father's library,' Peter said. 'His are mostly in Greek or Latin, and the rest are sermons or theology. This one is mine. But I have others—a few. If you have read this one would you rather have Hadslypt's *Voyages*? Though I've only got one volume of that.'

Tom Wildgoose shook his head, 'There are times when old friends make the best company. And I know of few better for my present needs than Cervantes. Thank you, I will take the greatest care of him.'

And it was Peter who a few days later, cut him a stout blackthorn staff to help him get back onto his feet again.

Damaris, arriving later on the same afternoon, found him hobbling about Joyous Gard leaning on it. At some time while he was ill, Genty had washed his shirt for him, and sponged and mended the knee of his breeches, so that he really looked quite respectable; but the first thing she noticed as he straightened up and turned to face her, was his height. Never having seen him on his feet before, she had not thought of him as tall, only long. Now she checked, looking at him with surprised interest. 'How tall you are! It's a good thing you're narrow, or we would never have got you across Snowball's back on the day we found you!'

'It's a good thing I'm narrow,' he agreed, and took a hobbling step towards her.

'Ought you to be walking yet?' Damaris asked doubtfully.

'No,' said Genty's voice in the doorway, 'he shouldn't.' And the Wise Woman came in and set down the usual basket that she carried. 'Not for so many days as there are fingers on my liddle ol' left hand with the thumb turned down.' She turned on Tom like a small scolding game-hen, 'Haven't 'ee no sense in that thick high head of yours, my fine young gentleman? Do 'ee want the wound breaking down, or the fever back again?'

'No more than any man would,' said Tom Wildgoose, 'but I am being careful, and it's time to get some practice in—I must be on my way before many more days are out. Look, I'll sit down now, if it will stop you scolding.' And he folded up onto the piled bracken of his bed, laying his staff beside him.

'Where must you be away to?' Damaris asked, not looking at him. She had not asked until then, but his going away had not seemed so suddenly near, before.

'London,' he said, 'and then back to—where I came from.'

'And how would 'ee be thinking of gettin' to London?' asked Genty, unpacking her basket. 'Will 'ee add horse thievin' to smugglin'?'

He shook his head. 'No need. I've enough gold in my purse for the stage coach—just about. And once I get there, I have friends.'

'Well, ye'll not go anywhere till the moon's past its first quarter,' Genty told him. 'Now pull down that stocking and I'll take a look how the wound does.'

Chapter 7: Mr Farrington's Hunting

The moon was not far off Genty's first quarter; or it would be when evening came and you could see it. Now it was afternoon, and Damaris was sitting with Tom Wildgoose in the doorway of Joyous Gard. The first real warmth of the year was in the sunshine, and Tom had left his jacket on the piled bracken of his bed. Earlier, he had been practising walking in the little tangled clearing and along the edge of the rife, even managing short distances without his blackthorn staff. Earlier, too, Peter had been with them, but he had had to go home a while since, because his Great Aunt was coming on a visit, and at such times he was always expected to be there and make a good impression so that Great Aunt would continue to help with his school fees. Peter was not very interested in his school fees, but he realized that the stipend of a country vicar was not large, especially in a lean year when everybody tried to get out of paying their tithes; also he liked his Great Aunt, who had never had any sons of her own, and knew that she would be hurt if he was not there to greet her. So he had gone off with a slightly ill grace, and now the other two sat by themselves in the ramshackle doorway of Joyous Gard.

All about them the Manhood was waking up to the spring-time, the sky as blue as a dunnock's egg beyond the interlacing twigs of the still bare trees, and all the mazy woodlands alive with the flitter of small birds. All so safe and peaceful that looking about her and listening to the Manhood thrush singing his soul out nearby, Damaris could scarcely believe in the other darker things that went on among the same woods and along the same marshy coast; in the cross on the stable door and Shadow Mason playing 'Spanish Ladies' in the lane, and the snapping of pistol shots in the night that had brought Tom Wildgoose into their lives. Easier to believe in this morning's dark thing; the news that a fox had taken two of the Big House peahens that one heard sometimes screaming before rain. She was sure that it could not have been Lady's doing, though nobody else would have shared her certainty; but the big dog fox was another matter, and whichever of them was the killer, it could mean danger for Lady, just the same. . . .

Tom Wildgoose was sitting with his head tipped back against the half-rotten doorpost, his gaze moving in a lingering sort of way over the clearing before them. 'I suppose you know these woods better than almost anyone,' he said, 'you and Peter, and Genty Small.'

Damaris nodded. 'There's the Gypsies of course.'

'Are there Gypsies in the Manhood?'

'Not now. Later in the year they come, around harvest time.' Damaris linked her hands round her up-drawn knees. The memory of the big dog fox on the edge of the clearing, with the sunlight turning his red-brown to flame was weaving thought-links in her head, and suddenly for the moment she was not seeing the spring-time woods at all. 'Two years ago when I was ten there was a gypsy girl came and danced in the tithe barn at harvest supper. She had a flame-coloured petticoat; silky—it made a rustling sound like taffeta—swirling out round her on the threshing floor; and all the lanterns were lit, and the fiddler playing, and stars seemed to be dancing too in the open doorway. And afterwards everything seemed dull and ordinary for a while, and there was not anything I wanted in the world so much as a flame-coloured taffeta petticoat. But nobody understood.'

'Nobody ever does,' said Tom Wildgoose, sadly. 'And now that you are twelve and almost grown up, do you still want a flame-coloured taffeta petticoat?'

Damaris met his look gravely. 'Yes. But I don't tell people about it anymore. That is—I don't know why I told you.'

Tom Wildgoose was silent a long moment. Then he said, 'Maybe because I'm just someone passing through. I'll soon be away, so it doesn't really matter.'

Damaris shook her head. 'I know you'll soon be away, but you're not just someone passing through—Oh Tom, I shan't ever forget you!'

He smiled, 'Nor shall I ever forget you, any of you, Peter or Genty—or Damaris—or these English woods with the sea sounding in them. . . .'

'Don't! You sound as though you were going so far away,' said Damaris with a small catch in her voice.

And then screwing up her courage, she asked, 'Tom, will you write to me, sometimes?'

'No,' said Tom Wildgoose.

'But if you don't send me word, I shan't know, ever—where you are, or how you are—or—'

Tom Wildgoose brought his gaze back from the tree-tops. 'When you come to be married, I will send you a length of flame-coloured taffeta for a petticoat to wear under your wedding-dress. And when you get it, you will know that all is well with me and I wish you happy.'

Damaris sat looking down at her hands. 'You will not know when I come to be married.'

'I'll know. News travels on the smuggling luggers for anyone who—takes an interest.'

They were silent again.

And in the silence suddenly the woods were uneasy.

Knowing them as she did, Damaris felt the uneasiness before she saw or heard anything to account for it. Then as she listened, head up like a woodland creature herself, the waiting quiet was torn apart by the alarm call of a jay. And a few moments later, faint and far off and gone again almost before she caught it, the musical menace of hounds giving tongue.

'What is it?' Tom asked.

'Hounds, I think. Mr Farrington at the Big House has a kind of rough pack of them, all kinds, five or six. And sometimes he takes it into his head to hunt something, 'specially when his London friends are down with him.' The cold shadow of fear that had been at the back of her mind all day suddenly took shape, and she gripped her hands together. 'A fox took two of the Big House peahens last night—'

Almost as she spoke, the baying of hounds broke out again nearer this time, and a moment later a moving flicker of red showed among the under-growth at the edge of the clearing, and a young vixen arrowed out from the brambles, hard-pressed and with panting flanks, and made for the cottage as for a remembered refuge.

'Lady!' Damaris gasped, as the red shadow streaked in through the open doorway between her and Tom. 'But she couldn't have! It must have been the dog fox!'

Both of them were on their feet, Tom with his blackthorn staff suddenly become a weapon in his hands. 'It makes no difference which of them. It's *her* scent they have,' he snapped. 'Get inside after her.'

'I'll stay with you—'

'*Get inside*,' Tom said in the kind of voice one did not argue with. 'And pile everything you can against the door after you.'

The dogs were quite close, and the woods were wild with the shouting of men and the yelp of a hunting horn. Damaris sprang back into the thick shadows, and Tom heaved the half-rotten door to behind her. 'Whatever happens stay there and do not make a sound.' She heard his voice through the timbers. 'You could have the smell of fox on you.'

Half sobbing, she heaved the heavy log they used as a table across the door, and jammed it with a fallen branch they had been going to use for a new roof beam, by and by—Lady was somewhere behind her, crouched back into the darkest corner. She could hear the vixen's terrified panting, and something of the same fear was in herself. Mr Farrington's dogs knew her and she them, but she had never before met them running loose as a pack on the hunting trail; but more than for herself she was afraid for Lady, and for Tom Wildgoose with his blackthorn staff, in the doorway, who they did not know at all.

Her heart drubbing in the base of her throat, she

ran to the narrow window-hole, and peered out through the dense tangle of ivy and traveller's joy that curtained it over. Squinting sideways she could get a glimpse of Tom standing before the door; and next instant half-a-dozen hounds broke from cover, and on their heels young Mr Farrington winding his hunting horn and clad in an outlandish bright yellow coat trimmed with silver lace. She did not notice the coat at the time, but the odd thing was that she remembered it ever afterwards. And a couple of his London friends and Matthew Binns, all giving tongue like their ill-assorted pack.

She could not see much of what happened after that, it was just a shapeless, ugly swirl of sound and movement, men shouting, the baying of the hounds taking on a snarling note. She heard Mr Farrington shouting 'Stand away from that door!' And something about a fox that had killed his peafowl.

And Tom shouting back in a queer broken accent not at all like his own, 'Ze fox, 'e is not 'ere, 'e go that way—'

'You're lying!' Mr Farrington shouted, 'Or why are you guarding that door?'

'You startle me—I am sleeping and you come—' Tom began in the same odd accent; and then a horrible tangle of noise that seemed to crash and worry against the thin shell of refuge in which she and the vixen crouched. Then up from the turmoil she heard Tom cry out again, sharply like a man badly frightened, 'Sacré bleu!' And then a whole string of foreign words falling over each other and mixed with English ones in the same foreign accent. 'I tell you ze fox'e go that way—ah, mon dieu! Call off ze dogs, zey kill me!'—

There was a bellow of laughter from Mr Farrington, ''Tis a Frenchman, egad! We started out after a fox and we've caught a Froggie spy!'

'Well ye can't blame the dogs,' somebody else shouted. 'All the monsieurs stink as high as any fox, and the poor beasts couldn't tell the difference!'

But at least the turmoil was growing less, and Matthew Binns seemed to be whipping off the dogs.

Tom Wildgoose was protesting furiously, but in a way that somehow did not sound like the truth, 'I am not a spy! I am honest seaman; I mees my sheep!'

'Unless she's a smuggling craft, you've wandered a long way in searching for her,' Mr Farrington whooped, and there was a splurge of laughter.

'Well whatever he is, he's up to no good, Sir,' put in Matthew Binns, who had got the dogs back under control. 'Been in a brush of some sort, too, by the look of his knee.'

They all looked at Tom's knee, where he still had to wear his breeches tied loose over the bandage that showed underneath. 'Aye, you're in the right of it, Binns.' Mr Farrington sobered up somewhat, and grew interested. 'Tie his hands behind him, and we'll get him back to the house. We can lodge him in the stables for the night, and find out who he is and just what he *has* been up to in the morning—Run him up before the magistrates in Chichester if need be.' Laughter overcame him again. 'Hang him with any luck!'

To Damaris, still clinging to what remained of the window-ledge everything had gone unreal; and when in a little while, with the hounds in leash, the hunting party turned back on its tracks, the sight of Tom with his hands lashed behind him, stumbling along in their midst on his wounded knee, seemed the most unreal of all, like something in a bad dream.

Only it was not a dream.

The sounds of their going died away. Only somewhere far off she heard again the alarm call of a jay to tell where they went by. And after that only the familiar sounds of the Manhood and the faint hushing of the incoming tide.

Damaris stayed by the window a short while longer; shivering with the shock of it all, and utterly bewildered as to why Tom should have led Mr Farrington and his friends to think that he might be a French spy. She remembered Mr Farrington's laughter, 'Hang him, with any luck!' and she felt coldly sick. Why, why had he done such a crack-brained thing? And the answer came to her. He had done it to save her and Lady. He must have known that he could not hold them off for long, that the dogs would have the ramshackle door down and find her and the vixen, and she knew enough of hounds at the kill to know that unless the hunting party took in what was happening and were very quick to the rescue, she must have been in almost as hideous danger as Lady. He had to give them something that would seem to them more interesting than a cornered fox to set their minds going in another direction, gambling on being able to get himself out of the tangle later. But how if he could not? How if they would not believe he had only been out to save the fox? That alone would infuriate them; and why *should* they believe? It seemed an unlikely enough story. And come to that, who *was* Tom, and what *had* he been up to? Was it something they might hang him for anyway, if they found out about it?

Her thoughts were racing round and round inside her head like scurrying mice in a cage. But in a little, the ones that mattered shook themselves clear of the scurry and stood clear above the rest. For whatever reason Tom had run himself into danger, tonight he would be locked up in the Big House stables, waiting for whatever tomorrow might throw at him, and somehow he must be rescued before tomorrow came.

She stopped shaking and got to her feet, and heaved

aside the log and the fallen branch from behind the door. A long last moment, she stood listening; then she pulled the door open. As she did so, a red shadow slipped free of the other shadows in the far corner, and was gone past her into the hazy evening sunshine and the mazy shadows beyond the clearing.

Lady had gone to her own world, and this time she would not come back again. The magic circle was broken.

Chapter 8: The Wicked Thing

Damaris had no need to wonder this time who she should go to for help. No use going to the Vicarage, as she had done on the day, now seemingly so long ago, when she had found her smuggler lying face down among the dog's mercury; there would be no possibility of Peter getting away this evening without somebody asking disastrous questions. That left only one person to turn to; and she set off for Genty's cottage. Snowball would just have to bide where he was for a while, she would be quicker without him. But when her hurried way brought her past the usual place where she had left him hitched, he was not there; and the trampled grass and torn-off willow catkins told their own story. The noise of the hunt must have startled him, and he had dragged free and bolted.

She checked a moment, considering. Actually, it might be a good thing. Snowball would take himself home, and they would be frightened at Carthagena. She was sorry about that. Also of course it would start them looking for her, which was a pity. But it would give her a good excuse if she needed one, for being out late; for she could say that the hunt had startled him (that bit would be true, anyway) while she was looking for primroses, and she had been looking for him ever since. That might mean that they would forbid her to go off on her own for a while. But when you had a lot of problems on your hands the best you could so was to take them one at a time.

She was already running again, her skirts bunched inelegantly to her knees. Branches whipped across her face, brambles like witches' fingers clutched hold of her, and she left wisps of dark green worsted here and there in her wake. And as she had done that other time, she was praying as she ran, that she might find Genty at home; for if she didn't, she could not think what she was to do.

She was only just in time, for when she reached the cottage in its woodshore clearing just short of the village, the Wise Woman had her cloak on and was stowing things in her basket on the table, while the little grey cat sat watching her from the window-sill.

'What is it, then?' she asked, as Damaris almost fell down the step into the strange-smelling room. And while Damaris poured out her story, she went on filling the basket.

Damaris was not even sure that she was listening properly; but when all was told, the old woman said, 'Aye—in the stable, ye say? Then Mus' Binns will be our man, my lover.'

'Then you'll go to the Big House? You'll go now?'

Genty had turned to the carved old chest under the window and opened it, speaking with her head half inside, 'Not I, my lover. There'a a child down at the fisher cottages needs me tonight, more'n your Tom Wildgoose.'

'But Genty—Oh you must help him, you *must*!'

Genty had opened the painted leather box from which she had taken her surgeon's tools, that other night, the box where she had said she kept her 'Wicked Things'. 'And let the child die? No, no, there's a better way than that.'

'But if you will not come—'

'I said I wouldn' come, I didn' say I wouldn' help the lad.' Genty closed the box, then let down the lid of the chest carefully as though there were eggs within, and turned round with something in her hand. Damaris could not see what it was, for the shadows were gathering in the little crowded room. 'But 'tis you that must carry my help to the right person and set it working. Now listen: Mus' Binns will be at supper in his own cottage by now, an' away back to the stables afore long, so 'ee must be quick to catch him on his own. Tell him I sent 'ee, and ask him to arrange for the 'scape of the lad they took by mistake for a fox this afternoon.'

Was that all Genty with her strange powers could suggest? 'He won't,' Damaris said desperately, 'Why should he? Not just for asking—when it might mean trouble for him?'

Genty nodded, 'Indeed I think a' won't, just for asking. But, 'tis only courteous to ask, first. 'Tis clumsy way o' doin' things, to start wi' a threat, afore 'tis certain-sure one's needed.'

'A threat?' said Damaris.

The Wise Woman set down a little bundle on the table, and folded back the corners of the kerchief in which it was wrapped. Damaris saw a heart roughly shaped in wax, about the size of the palm of her hand or maybe a little larger. The thing looked innocent enough, but Genty had something else in the hollow of her other hand. Five long blackthorn spines. She picked up the heart, and deliberately and precisely drove the thorns into it.

Damaris watched her with widening eyes, seeing the thing in her hand change its nature and become suddenly evil. She had always known, of course, that Genty and her kind had other skills than medicine and the making of herb cheese and Sunday love charms—she had heard the maids whispering over their work—but she had never come in contact with this darker side of Genty's skills before.

The Wise Woman folded the little bundle up again. 'If the threat be needed, then show him this, and tell him that ol' Genty bade you, and that she has another the like of this one, wi' his name writ on it fair, an' blackthorn spines are easy come by.'

Damaris's throat felt tight. 'And—will he believe—believe—' she managed, but could get no further.

The Wise Woman smiled; a small inward turning smile. 'Aye, he'll believe. Mus' Binns is the best Horse Master in these parts. He has the power of the Toad Bone that floats upstream; he knows the Words, and the Secrets of Control. He knows enough of his own skills to be afeared o' mine.' She held out the bundle, 'Take it, and be away with 'ee.'

Damaris drew back a pace. It seemed to her that the shadows were crowding thicker in the corners of the room. 'I—Genty, I can't!' she whispered.

'There is no harm in it: I have not spoken the Words, I have not made the Signs, I have not mingled the dark-of-the-Moon herbs. 'Tis but a warning.'

Damaris half-reached out, then drew back her

hand. She was more frightened of the thing Genty held than she had ever been of anything before. She looked up desperately into the old woman's face.

'Be 'ee still so feared?' Genty said. 'Then listen, my Lover, for 'tis as simple as this: if you cares enough what comes to this Tom Wildgoose of your'n, take this and get him free. If you don't, then leave be, and go away. Like enough, they'll not get to hangin' him, anyways.'

And Damaris put out her hand, and took the little bundle. It felt very cold, and surprisingly heavy. She knew that she was handling something much better left alone. She was as frightened as ever. But it was that or deserting Tom. . . .

'What must I do after that?' she said. Her mouth felt dry.

Genty had already turned back to her basket, and was spreading a clean white cloth over the things within. 'That be for you an' Mus' Binns to arrange a'tween you,' she said. 'But mind, the lad can't go back to your Joyous Gard—Can 'ee get out o' the house after you're supposed to be in bed for the night?'

'Yes, Genty.'

'Good. Then bid Mus' Binns to have the lad out by Dame's Folly across the house paddock, at whatever time seems good to both of 'ee. Do you be waiting for him, an' bring him on here. I shall still be away down to the fisher cottages, for 'tis sure to be an all-night sitting; but my door is ever on the latch as you do know.' She was putting a loaf and a jug on the table as she spoke, followed by a candle and the household tinder-box. 'Bid him eat, and sleep by the fire till I come. Then get yourself 'long home.'

'And this?' Damaris moved the little bundle.

'Leave it on the mantel for me, here.' Genty picked up the basket and turned to the door. 'Now go, for

70

the child's needs are calling me, an' I've no more time to spare.'

A few minutes later Damaris was coming up to the back gate of Matthew Binns's cottage that opened onto the common at the far end of the village. She was wondering how she was to get word with him apart from his wife, but luck was with her for just as she got there, he appeared from the direction of the Big House stables, and she realized that he must have only just done with getting the prisoner locked up, and be coming home late to his supper.

She stepped out from the shadow of the hedge into his path. In the fading light and with her hood pulled well forward, he did not recognize her, but gave her a grunted greeting as though she were one of the village girls, and made to pass her by. She slipped round to be still between him and the gate. 'I'll not keep you for long from your supper, Mus' Binns, but I've a message for you from Genty Small.'

He sounded faintly startled, 'That ol' hag? What do she want wi' me?'

Damaris took a deep breath. 'She wants, if you please, that you should arrange the 'scape of the lad you took by mistake for a fox this afternoon.'

He let out a ragged breath, 'What lad would that be, then?'

'The one you have shut up in the stables,' Damaris said firmly.

'How in the world—' Mr Binns began, and then changed direction. 'An' what makes Genty Small think as I'll do tha-at, just for the askin'?'

'Because of this,' Damaris felt her mouth shaking, but she managed to keep her voice steady, as she brought the small bundle from under her cloak and unfolded the wax heart. There was enough light to show it, palely ugly, and with the five dark thorns stuck deep in it. It was all she could do not to throw

71

the thing on the ground. There was utter silence; and when she looked up, Matthew Binns's face had taken on much the same waxy paleness as the small wicked thing in her hand, which he was staring at as though he could not move his eyes away.

'What do she want him for?'

'I don't know.'

'Take un away,' he muttered.

'There's no harm in it,' Damaris told him, in the same carefully steadied voice. 'Not in this one. But she bade me tell you that she has another with your name writ on it fair, and blackthorn spines are easy come by.'

Matthew Binns wiped the back of his hand across his forehead, and she saw the sweat gleaming on it.

''Twill cost me my job.'

'I should not think so. Not if you're careful,' Damaris said; and then very softly, 'Genty says that you are the best Horse Master in these parts. She says that you have the Power of the Toad Bone that floats upstream, and you know Words, and the Secrets of Control. She says that you know enough of your own skills to be afraid of hers.' She did not know that she was sounding so unlike herself that Matthew Binns was never afterwards sure who had brought him the Wise Woman's message, but had a cold feeling that it was something Genty had called up for the purpose, out of the woods and the twilight.

He gave a kind of sick gulp. 'Curses on the old besom!—Aye, I'll do it. Only take that thing away!'

Damaris wrapped the wax heart up again and took it back under her cloak. 'Thank you,' she said politely. 'At what o'clock will you have him free?'

'How should I know?' Mr Binns seemed bolder with the heart out of sight. 'Isn't it enough that I get him free?'

'No,' Damaris made a movement under her cloak to bring it out again.

'Midnight,' he said hurriedly. 'No, that's too early. By one in t' morning Mus' Farrington an' his cronies will be too drunk to see straight, wi' any luck. One o'clock, then.'

'At one o'clock have him at Dame's Folly.'

'Anything more?' said Matthew Binns, savagely.

'No, nothing more. The kindness of the Good Folk on your supper.'

She never knew what had made her say that. She saw him go through the gate and up his path, a little unsteadily. Then she turned and ran.

Chapter 9: 'Dame's Folly'

When she got home, after a hurried pause to hide the wax heart among the roots of the tamarisk hedge (nothing on earth would have induced her to bring it into the house), Snowball had arrived before her, and the place was in a turmoil and her father and the farmhands were again making ready to set out on the search for her.

She told the story she had ready, but it was not well received. 'This,' said her father, 'is getting to be too much of a habit with you, my girl. If you cannot be trusted to come home at the proper time, you had best not go out alone until you can!'

That was what Damaris had been afraid of. She gathered herself together and stood up to him squarely. 'I know that last time I forgot the hour, Father, but this is different. You told me yourself that you must—must take *responsibility* for any animal that belongs to you, or—or that you have power over. Would you have liked me just to come home leaving Snowball lost in the woods?'

'Snowball was no more lost than you are!' said her exasperated father. 'He came home as straight as a bullet!'

'He wasn't heading for home when I last saw him, Father, he was making towards the Big House—but in the end when I had quite lost him, I thought it would be best to come home and ask Caleb to go and look for him; and then when I got home he had arrived before me and if he frightened everybody, Father, I am truly sorry, but you do see—'

'Yes, I do see.' John Crocker cut into the spate of words and somehow, having once started, she had seemed unable to stop. 'Well, now that you *are* home, perhaps we can have supper. But first, upstairs with you and see your Aunt; you have brought on one of her headaches as well as setting the whole farm by the ears. I hope you are proud of yourself!'

At bed-time, with Aunt Selina still having her headache, Damaris knelt by her bed to say her prayers with all her clothes still on. To undress would only have meant getting dressed again later. So, though she did not wish Aunt Selina one of her headaches, she could not be really sorry that if she was going to have one, it should be tonight that she had it.

She took longer about her prayers than usual, and prayed much more deeply and earnestly, because the wax heart with the five blackthorn spines on it stuck in the back of her mind like the taste of something horrible clinging round the back of one's throat. She had been mixed up with something that might very likely make God angry with her. But she was quite clear in her mind that whatever wickedness she had done, she would have done far worse to have left Tom Wildgoose to risk being hanged as a French spy. She explained this humbly but firmly to God, thinking it out and getting it straight within herself as she went along. Finally she asked forgiveness for whatever He might feel needed forgiving. Then she got up and sat on her bed and waited.

She was sure that she did not have to worry about keeping awake; she had never felt so far from sleep in all her life. She had not been able to eat much of her supper, and now she felt both hungry and a little sick, and shivery with that odd shiveriness that had nothing to do with being cold.

She almost did fall asleep once or twice, all the same, but each time jerked awake again; then she would get up and walk round the room on her stockinged feet before going back to sit on her bed again.

She watched the candle on her bedside table, which normally Aunt Selina would have taken away, burn low into its socket and start to jump and gutter, sending tall fantastic shadows leaping up the walls, until she had to blow it out and sit in the dark. She heard her father coming to bed in the room across the corridor, and the sounds of the old house settling down, and very faint and far off the Church clock striking 9–10–11–. She felt, as time crawled by, as though she had got trapped somehow in a night that was never going to be over and let her out into the morning.

At last the distant clock struck twelve, and something inside her tightened at the sound. Time to be moving. If she was too early at the meeting place she could wait there instead of here.

She took down her cloak from its hook behind the door, and put it on, tying the neck-strings with a small determined tug, and carrying her shoes in her hand, slipped out into the corridor, inching her door to behind her. Faint starlight on the old polished boards showed her the head of the stairs, and she crept down, taking care to miss out the third step from the bottom which always creaked when you trod on it. She felt for the clutter of sticks and cudgels and a shepherd's crook that stood in the corner by the house doorway, and found a stout ashen thumb-stick of her father's which he seldom used and with luck would not miss for a while, and got it out with infinite care not to bring the rest clattering down after it, and headed for the great flagged kitchen and the door into the dairy yard. The bar was up as usual at night, but that was easily lifted and laid aside, and she crept out, pulling the door to quietly behind her.

True, the yard dog, came out of his kennel by the stable archway, yawning his pleasure, to greet her, 'She-sh!' Damaris whispered, rubbing his warm rough neck, 'it's only me; I'll be back soon. Go sleep now.' And as True returned to his warm straw, she ran barefoot through the wicket gate into the lane and round to the front of the house, and felt among the roots of the tamarisk hedge for the little bundle she had left there. Her hand flinched from the feel of it, and it was all she could do to pick it up again; but she managed it, and stowed it in the pocket of her apron so as to have enough hands to spare for her shoes and the thumb-stick.

Then she set off in the direction of the village.

At a safe distance from the house she sat in the hedge and put on her shoes, then she went on again. She had never been abroad in the middle of the night before, and the familiar country seemed strange under the stars, and the sound of the sea much nearer than usual. Once a barn owl on the hunting trail floated across her path ghostwise on pale furred wings and a few moments later she heard the tiny shriek of a woodmouse. The night-time woods were up and hunting. Once she heard the uncanny scream of a vixen a long way off, but that was not hunting, that was Lady calling her mate, and somewhere further off still, a dog-fox barked twice in reply. But apart from stumbling into a ditch that was not there in the daytime, she met with no adventures or mishaps until she arrived at last, over beyond the village, at the little, neglected Folly, and stood looking across the home paddock to the Big House beyond its screening ilex trees.

She was ahead of time, she thought, and sat down on the step, leaning against one of the pillars. (The Folly had been built like a tiny Roman temple by an earlier Mrs Farrington who had once been to Italy and was, like Aunt Selina, of a romantic disposition.) Damaris pulled her cloak round her, and settled herself to wait.

In a while she became aware that something was happening over beyond the ilex trees. Lights were coming and going in the direction of the stable yard, and she caught a distant flurry of voices and the shrill squealing of an angry horse; and for a moment she thought there was a red flicker behind the roofs. But that was gone before she could be sure she hadn't imagined it. What, oh what was happening over there? Had something gone dreadfully wrong? The church clock struck one, the lights and the small tumult were fading out. Whatever had happened, it was over.

The minutes crawled by; still nothing; would Tom never come?

And then suddenly he was there; a black shadow travelling at a desperate kind of running hobble, pitching down in the black shadow of the crazy little temple, and lying there drawing in great shuddering gulps of air.

Damaris let him get his breath back a little before she spoke; then she whispered, 'It's all right, it's only me. We'll stay here till you have your breath properly back, but then I think we ought to go.'

He broke off between one snatched breath and the next, and there was a moment of startled silence. 'Good God! Is it you, Damaris?'

'Yes. Oh Tom, what has been happening back there?'

'I'm not too sure. Some cursed high-mettled horse had a fit of the vapours, I think, and—tried to kick his stall down, and a lantern—got overturned. Someone let me out—maybe they thought the stable might go up—and drew the line at roasting even French spies. There was a side door open and—somebody pushed me through and said something about making for the building at the far corner of the paddock—' He broke off and sat up on the step. 'Damaris, what *are* you doing here?'

'Genty couldn't come. She had to go to a sick baby, so I came to meet you and take you to her cottage.'

'Then you—you know about all this?'

'Yes—but I think we should go now.'

'I'm sure you're right,' said Tom Wildgoose. 'But I don't think I'm going to be a very good traveller, not without my staff.'

'We'll get it tomorrow,' Damaris told him. 'Till then—it's not far to Genty's cottage, and I've brought you Father's thumb-stick—here it is.'

He gave a croak of laughter. 'What a girl you are! Think of everything!' He fumbled for it in the dark as she held it out to him, and got up, steadying himself against the nearest pillar. 'Ah, that's better . . . Now, which way?'

It took them some time to skirt the village, for Tom was slow and clumsy on his wounded knee, even with the thumb-stick, and Damaris moving ahead to keep him out of ditches and find the weak places in hedgerows for him; and all the while she was terrified that the noise they made would set the village dogs barking.

But they got safely to Genty's cottage at last. It was dark and humped like a large sleeping hedgehog in its little woodshore clearing, but the door was on the latch, and Damaris found the tinder-box on the table and lit the candle beside it. The light sprang up long and ragged, and all the bundles of herbs and roots and dried things hanging from the ceiling and the jars and baskets and nameless masses lining the walls sent up leaping shadows in answer, shadows that might hide almost anything or grow long-fingered hands and take on shapes of their own at any moment. Damaris turned to the window and pulled the rough wooden shutter across, shutting out the crowding trees together with any curious eyes that might come peering in. When she looked round again, the candle-flame had steadied into the proper laurel leaf shape, blue at the heart and saffron fringed, that candle flames should be, and the shadows had shrunk back into their proper shapes and their proper places, and the room had taken on a look of kindness and shelter. The loaf and the jug stood ready on the table, Grizelda sat on the gay rag rug before the banked-down fire, her eyes shining like green-gold lamps. And Tom Wildgoose was leaning on the thumb-stick and looking dazedly about him.

Damaris saw that he was so tired that she was going to have to take charge and tell him exactly what to do. She pulled the chair round to the table. 'Now sit down and eat that bread, and here's milk. And then get some sleep in front of the fire. Remember to blow out the candle when you have done eating. Genty will be back, but I don't know when. Wait till she comes.'

He let himself down into the chair like an old man.

Damaris had taken the little wax effigy from her pocket, and was reaching up to stow it behind a crock on the chimney-piece. When she turned round, he was lying forward with his arm on the table and his head on his arm. Like enough he would sleep like that all night and never touch the bread or milk. Well, the food was there if he wanted it.

'I have to go now, Tom Wildgoose,' she whispered. She blew out the candle herself, and leaving the cottage dark save for the faint glow of the banked fire, set off for home.

She was beginning to feel that the woods were criss-crossed with the tracks of all these comings and goings like the wildling tracks in the grass on frosty mornings. And the way seemed very long. But she came at last, her shoes once again in her hand, up the lane beside Carthagena and across the yard to the side door. She had a bad moment, imagining that her father or somebody else might have chanced to come down and found the door unfastened and put up the bar again. But when she raised the latch it swung open easily enough, and she slipped through into the warm familiarity of home, leaving the strangeness of the night behind her. She crept upstairs, mindful of the third step from the bottom, past the door of the chamber where Aunt Selina was snoring gently, and back in the safety of her own small room, just managed to pull off her cloak and gown, leaving them both lying on the floor, and fall into bed before sleep engulfed her.

Chapter 10: Her Majesty's Customs

Surprisingly, Damaris did not oversleep next morning. After only three or four hours' sleep, she woke up gummy-eyed and still leaden with tiredness, but at the usual time, as though something in her had remembered, even while she slept, that the events of the past days were not yet over, and she must be stirring again before anything else could happen while she was not there.

Aunt Selina was still stretched upon her bed, moaning faintly with her bottle of Hungary Water in her hand, when Damaris having brushed the worse of last night's mud off her skirts, looked in on her. No lessons today.

She ran downstairs and out of the house. She

longed to be away instantly to the Wise Woman's cottage. But her sense told her that if she was missing at breakfast time, after what had happened the evening before, her father really would begin to suspect that something very odd was going forward, and then he would certainly put his foot down and refuse to let her go out alone. It might even end in a beating, which she would not so much mind, for he could never bring himself to lay it on properly, and in being locked in her room, which would be a disaster. So she stuck her head into the stable to see that all was well with Snowball, and found the pony comfortable and contented in his stall, alone save for her father's Swallow, for Caleb and Dick with the farm horses were already about the day's work. Waiting only to give both of them a bit of carrot, she darted off to pay a call on the lambing fold and see what newcomers there were since yesterday.

The barn fold was full of woolly backs and up-raised heads, the air bubbling with the shrill cries of the new lambs and the deep fond bleating of their mothers. Sim Bundy was busy at the far end of the fold, and so, unexpectedly, was Peter. He grinned when he saw her, and came wading towards her through the sea of bobbing fleeces, taking care to make no sudden movement to startle the sheep.

'I came to see if the wall-eyed ewe had dropped her lamb in the night,' he said, moving aside the gate-hurdle and coming out to join her. 'Sim was afraid she might have trouble, but she's well enough, and she's dropped a fine little ewe lamb.'

'You sound like a shepherd yourself,' Damaris told him. But she saw in his face that something was wrong, and drew him round the corner of the barn. 'What is it?'

'Tom's gone,' he said, 'I looked in on my way here, and he's not at Tumbledown, and he hasn't taken his jacket with him and his staff's lying before the doorway. And there's some crazy story all over the village that Mr Farrington had a French spy locked up in the stables, and Lucifer went wild in the night and kicked his stall to pieces and overset a lantern. And the spy got out in all the garboil and disappeared—'

'I know,' Damaris checked his quick anxious flow of words. 'I'll tell you all about it later. But he's all right; he's at Genty's cottage.'

He glared at her, 'What in Heaven's name's been happening? What have you been up to?'

'I *said* I'll tell you later. Now you'd best come in and have breakfast: if you've been here helping Sim with the ewes it will look more natural that way. Come on.' And she caught him by the hand and began dragging him back towards the house.

Half-an-hour later, with a good breakfast of bread and cheese and cold bacon inside them, they got up from the scrubbed kitchen table, and Damaris collected her cloak which she had flung across the back of a chair. Her father, pulling on his boots by the hearth while Hannah scrubbed pots and pans, cocked an eye at her. 'The fact that your Aunt Selina has one of her headaches need not mean that your education comes to a stop for the day, Dimmy. Is there naught that you can study by yourself? Couldn't you work on that fine ladylike sampler? Couldn't you at least help Hannah with the cooking or Madge in the dairy?'

Hannah let out a snort.

And Damaris protested hurriedly, 'Oh Father, Snowball needs exercise so badly! I think it was because I have not ridden him enough lately that he bolted yesterday.'

John Crocker pulled on the other boot, and looked at her consideringly, beginning to breathe loudly through his nose. Then he relented. 'Very well. But see that you don't have us taking search parties out after you, this time.'

'I won't. I promise.' Damaris stood on tiptoe and flung her arms round his neck, then darted out of the door. 'Come and help me saddle up,' she called to Peter as she passed him.

In the stable, with no human ears to hear them, she told him in a breathless rush all that had happened since he left Joyous Gard the day before. He whistled at the bit about the wax heart, and was inclined to be resentful at having missed it all, glaring at her across Snowball's back. 'I do say I think it a bit hard! I've taken my share of the dull jobs like keeping him fed all this while, and when something really exciting blows up, you have it all to yourself!'

'I didn't want it all to myself,' Damaris protested, beginning to lead Snowball out of his stall. 'Some of it was *too* exciting. But I couldn't come for you—you couldn't have come; not with your Great Aunt just arrived, not without people asking questions.'

'No, that's true—Oh well, it can't be helped.'

He gave her a heave into the saddle, and they clattered out of the yard, Peter with a hand on Snowball's rump.

At the edge of the woods they parted, Damaris riding on towards Genty's cottage, while Peter plunged off into the trees to collect Tom's jacket and blackthorn staff and bring them on.

There were constellations of celandines in the ditch that she had fallen into last night, and a flitter of yellow-hammers along the woodshore, and the black shadows of last night and the wicked little wax heart had fallen away behind her, because she had told Peter about it and so was not, as it were, shut up alone with it anymore. She had decided that it would be best to visit Genty quite openly as though on an errand for her aunt, this time. And so she rode Snowball through the tongue of woodland that shielded the Wise Woman's cottage from the lane, and slid from his good-natured back in the little clearing, hitching him to a hawthorn branch. A blue feather of smoke was rising from the chimney-hole, the white nanny was grazing comfortably in a patch of nettles, and the cottage looked its daytime self and as though it had never known a secret in all its life. Grizelda sat in the open doorway, washing herself with one hind leg pointing skyward like a flagpole. Damaris chirruped to her as she went in.

The cottage was full of pungent-smelling steam, and in the midst of the steam, Genty sat in her chair before the hearth with her skirts spread out round her and a shawl round her head, her feet in a great tub of hot herb-filled water, and another crock of hot water bubbling on the fire within easy reach.

Damaris checked in dismay, 'Genty, are you ill? Did you catch cold last night?'

'I'd not be surprised! but even a cold has its uses.' Genty looked up. 'Did 'ee see any strangers on the way here?'

'No. Why?'

'The village do be full o' Customs House men. Seems they're nosing round after some brandy or the like that they reckon is still hidden hereabouts, from the last Run.'

Damaris was glancing quickly and anxiously round the steam-filled cottage. As far as she could make out, the wax heart was gone from the place where she had left it; and she drew a quick breath of relief. She wanted never to see that terrible little image again. But nor was there any sign of Tom Wildgoose; and if there were Customs men about. . . . 'Where is he?' she asked. 'I left him here in the night.'

'Aye, so ye did my lover. And here I found him

safe and sleeping this morning. He's in a safe place, never you fret.'

Damaris was thinking suddenly of Peter heading this way with Tom's jacket and his empty pistol that he kept in its pocket. But he knew the Manhood, and had too much sense to run into riding-officers or any other of the Customs House men. And before she had time to say anything of this to Genty, she heard heavy footsteps on the grass path outside, and the Wise Woman's gaze flickered past her through the doorway. She made a quick warning movement of one hand, then lifted up her voice in a complaining snuffle. 'All night, I was with'un—Aye, the babe will do well enough, by God's Grace an' the power of ol' Genty's healing herbs, but what wi' getting drenched to the skin in the Church Dyke on the way back, I've all but caught my own death o' cold—' She sneezed explosively into a soggy handful of rags. 'Ye can see how 'tis wi' me, Liddle Mistress, an' no I've *not* yet made the freckle salve.'

Damaris, her back to the door, made signals of understanding with her eyebrows, and flounced down on a nearby stool. 'I'll wait,' she announced. 'Aunt said I was not to come back without it.'

The heavy footsteps had reached the door, and she looked round as a big man in the blue coat of the Customs service, with another, smaller and younger, at his heels, came down the step. Grizelda, pushed from her place, stalked off disdainfully, her tail erect behind her.

'An' who may you be, come pushing your way in here without so much as ' "with your leave" or a "by your leave"?' croaked Genty.

'Reckon you know that well enough, old mother,' said the big man. 'His Majesty's Customs, that's who I am.'

'Aye, so what do 'ee want wi' me?'

'A look round,' said the man, 'just a look round.'

''Ee can look till all's blue,' Genty snuffled. 'But ye'll not find aught as hasn't the right to be. If 'ee was wantin' a wart charmed, now, or mebbe a herb tussie-mussie to please a girl with. . . .'

The Customs man turned red. 'I ain't got no warts, an' I'm a respectable married man.'

'Married ye may be,' sniffed Genty. 'Respectable, never, not wi' a nose that colour.'

The younger man gave a snort of laughter, and turned it hurriedly into a cough.

'And you can shut your gob!' his senior rounded on him. Then, turning his attention back to Genty, 'Now that's enough o' that! Acting on Information Received that there's still contraband from the last Run hid somewhere hereabouts, we are here to search it out! Search it out, I say, wherever it may be. Even—,' he looked round him, 'in such a ramshackle birds' nest of a place as this.'

'Then ye'd better start searching,' said Genty with another sneeze. 'I'm sure *I'm* not stoppin' ye.'

'I shall, oh I shall, and don't think you can pull the wool over *my* eyes with this show of open doors and innocence!' He jerked his head in the direction of the ladder. 'You take the upstairs, Benjamin, and I'll have a look round here.'

Benjamin clumped away up the ladder, and they heard his boots overhead while the big man began to open cupboards and peer along shelves ('Try inside the salt crock,' said Genty.)

Damaris sat very still, her hands gripped together under her cloak, watching. Where was Tom? She was sure he was somewhere about, but there was no hiding-place except the tiny inner closet with slate shelves where Genty kept the milk and such of her remedies as needed to be kept cold. Maybe he was upstairs? Under Genty's bed? She heard Benjamin's boots going to and fro and the sound of furniture being pulled about. The big man heaved up the lid of the chest under the window and half disappeared inside it; and she held her breath. She knew Tom could not possibly be in there, but it had been from the painted leather box inside that chest that Genty had taken the little wax heart, and what else might he find in there of things that should not be seen? They did not burn witches nowadays, as far as she knew, but what about prison or transportation? She craned her neck to see past him into the darkness under the lid, but there was no box there, and as far as she could make out, the chest was almost empty.

The Customs House man slammed the lid down again, and turned away to peer up the chimney, almost upsetting the crock on the fire as he did so, despite Genty's warning screech; then, coughing and with watering eyes, he began to thump his way round the walls to hear if any of them rang hollow.

Benjamin's legs appeared through the hole in the ceiling. 'Nothing up there,' he reported, clambering down. 'Nor no one, neither.'

His senior grunted. 'Nothing here either.'

'Take a look outside?'

'Aye.'

They went out through the door, Genty squawking after them, 'If you're quite sure you've done wi' turning my house upsy down. . . .?'

For a short while Damaris sat rigid, looking at the Wise Woman, and listening to the Customs House men poking round in the wood-pile and thumping on the walls to see if they sounded any more hollow from outside. At last they seemed satisfied, and footsteps and grumbling voices departed, fading into the distance; the thrush that had been singing in the garden plot before they came returned to his singing, and Grizelda came stalking back to her place on the sun-warmed doorsill.

'Are they gone? I mean really gone?' Damaris asked.

'Reckon so. Give 'un a while longer to make sure.'

They waited; but the Customs House men did not come back to disturb the peace of the little clearing.

Genty pulled the shawl from her head and took her feet out of the tub of cooling water—Damaris noticed that hard and brown though they were, Genty had pretty feet, arched like a dancer's; like the gypsy dancer on the threshing floor at Harvest Home. She got up and shook out her skirts. Then she pulled her chair and the tub aside and flung back the hearth-rug. Under it, Damaris saw, was a trapdoor with a handle that lay flat in its own recess so there was no betraying lump under the hearth-rug once it was in place. Genty pulled up the trapdoor, revealing a small square of darkness. No, not quite darkness, for a faint glow like maybe the gleam of a rush-light seeped up from below. And with it Tom's voice asking in a hoarse whisper,

'Can I come up now, Genty?'

Chapter 11: A Time for Parting

'You'd best get down there an' keep him company for a while,' said Genty. 'He bain't all that happy down there shut in by hisself; but there he's got to stay while the daylight lasts—leastwise till the woods be clear of Customs House men, and your Mr Farrington's given up the idea of re-capturing his smuggler or French spy or whatever.'

By that time Damaris was peering down through the trap. A ladder ran down from it into the crowding shadows and the glim of the rush-light below; and as she looked, something moved and blotted out the glim, and she found herself almost nose to nose with Tom Wildgoose looking up at her.

'Hurry now,' said Genty's voice at her back, 'I don'

want to keep the trap open all day! But I'll be here close by to let 'ee out again, my lover.'

'Stand clear, I'm coming down,' Damaris said to the rather strained face with the forelock of dark hair drooping as usual across his forehead. She turned round and gathered her skirts close, and dropped through the hatch, feeling for the ladder below her. A hand came round her ankle and guided her foot to the rung, then the other foot. Then hands were round her waist, lifting her the rest of the way. The trapdoor dropped into place above her, and she turned to face the fugitive.

'I'll met by moonlight, proud Titania,' said Tom Wildgoose. 'Have you come to keep me from getting restive and clamouring to be let out at the wrong moment?'

Damaris nodded. 'How is your knee? You haven't made it worse?'

'*I* haven't made it worse,' said Tom meaningly. Then he grinned. 'It's doing well enough. My chief ailment at the moment is that I've no stomach for being mewed up in small dark places.'

'What *is* this place?' Damaris gazed about her at the baskets and bundles and hanging herb bunches. 'Genty's store-room, I suppose.' And then she realized that the far end of the narrow cellar was walled in with small round tubs that she knew well enough for brandy kegs, and her startled gaze flew back to Tom's face.

'Yes,' said Tom, 'it's someone else's store-room, as well as Genty's.'

After the first moment, Damaris was not really surprised. In smuggling country you never knew who was or was not mixed up with the Fair Traders (and all they had ever known about Genty in that way was that she would not care whether or not you were a smuggler if you needed her help), and a Wise

92

Woman's cottage would be a good place for a Hide, for folk would not in general be too keen to meddle with her or her belongings.

'Sit down, if you're going to stay a while,' said Tom, and sat down again himself on a square sacking-covered bale. Damaris sat down on its mate—all the bales and kegs were roped in pairs for carrying across a pack saddle or a man's shoulders. The flame of the rush-light guttered a little in the current of air from a small hole under the roof, which must come out somewhere at the back of the hearth in the room overhead. Like enough Tom Wildgoose wasn't the first man to have sheltered there while the search went by above him; and a man in hiding still needs air to breathe.

The flickering light woke and lost and woke again an answering yellow glint behind the foot of the ladder, and looking more closely, Damaris saw that it was the brass clasp of the painted leather box from which yesterday evening Genty had taken the terrifying little wax heart. No wonder she had not seemed at all worried about the Customs House man looking into the chest under the window. Damaris drew back a little, scarcely knowing that she did so, as though something in the box might leap out at her.

'It won't bite,' said Tom, noticing the direction of her gaze. 'I carried it down here when we heard the Customs House men were on the prowl—Look, no scorch marks,' he held out his hands.

Damaris gave a little shiver. 'Don't. You don't know what's in it.'

'I think I can guess, near enough. That little wax heart with the thorns in it that you left on the chimney-piece last night, when—I was pretty far gone, but not yet as deep into sleep maybe as you thought I was, that's in there, for one thing.'

'There wasn't any harm in that one,' Damaris said

quickly, telling herself as well as him. 'It hadn't got his name on it, and she hadn't spoken the Words, nor mingled the dark-of-the-moon herbs, she told me so.'

'So it was just for showing to someone? Up at the Big House? For a threat, maybe?'

'A warning, she called it.'

'A warning, then. I thought there was something odd about the way that stallion played up, and the lantern going over, and my prison door coming open in the midst of all the uproar.'

There was silence for a short while between them. Then Tom Wildgoose said, 'You must have been very much afraid, to carry the thing alone through the dark and use it, in whatever way you did use it, even though it *was* only a warning.'

Damaris said, giving him back look for look, 'I was afraid. But there wasn't any other way.'

He reached out and brushed his finger across her wrist, very lightly. 'There isn't really anything I can say, except "Thank you", is there, Damaris? No words beautiful and splendid and humble enough. If there were, I would say them all—'

Almost in the same instant they heard a murmur of voices overhead. The trapdoor lifted, and through the square of daylight came a pair of legs.

'Peter!' said Damaris.

He landed beside them, Tom's coat slung over his shoulder and the blackthorn staff in one hand. 'I'd have been here sooner,' he said, 'but I had to wait for the Customs House coves to have finished their poking and prying and be out of the way.' He grinned at Tom. 'It's my belief it wasn't only contraband they were after: what about that French spy who broke out of the Big House stables last night? With a wounded knee on him, he'd likely be lying up not far off.'

He and Tom were looking at each other steadily in the light of the tallow dip.

'If it was like that, why wouldn't they say it was the spy they wanted?' Damaris demanded (but she was suddenly remembering Benjamin coming down Genty's bedroom ladder, reporting 'Nothing up there. Nor no one, either').

Tom shrugged. 'Maybe this morning with a clearer head and a sorer one, young Mr Farrington isn't quite so sure that his prisoner *wasn't* just a French sailor who'd lost his ship, after all. And if *that* was the way of it, maybe he doesn't want to make himself look a worse fool than he does already, when a guinea in the hand of the Riding Officer may serve just as well.' He got up from the bale he was sitting on, and taking his jacket from Peter, began to shrug himself into it.

'And if they caught you for him?' Peter asked with interest, propping the blackthorn staff in a corner.

'I said he wouldn't want to look more of a fool than he does already. Perhaps he just wants to get me to Portsmouth or wherever my ship may be, before I can spread the tale. But I wouldn't care to wager on it.'

'Well, with any luck, we shall never know.' Peter had begun delving into his pockets. 'I thought it would be safer to put the things from your pockets into mine. Less likely to fall out—tinder-box—handkerchief, knife—' he passed the things over to Tom as he named them. 'Purse—pistol.'

Tom was stowing the things back into his own pockets. The purse he tossed up, listening to the rather faint chink of it. 'There's the price of my coach fare to London. Only one problem remains—how do I get to Chichester? He stowed the purse away. 'Stupid to be outfaced by a mere half-dozen miles of walking, but I don't think I can make it on foot.'

'You could wait for a few days longer?' Damaris pleaded.

And, 'The carrier goes up once a week, but he went

this morning,' said Peter. Both at the same instant.

Tom stowed the empty pistol in his pocket. 'No, I can't wait another week,' he said seriously. 'I am a danger to Genty while I hide here.' He sat down again on the bale and looked across at Peter squatting on the bottom rung of the ladder.

'Then what will you do?'

'I don't know as yet. I'll think of something—steal a horse, maybe.' He sobered suddenly. 'Peter, there's one thing more I have to ask of you: I have to go back to Joyous Gard, and I don't know the way.'

Peter nodded, 'The packet you had round your neck. I couldn't bring it—I didn't know where you'd hidden it.'

'No,' Tom said, 'I am the only one who knows that. Will you guide me back?'

'When?'

'It had better be tonight.'

'I shan't be able to get away much before half-past ten. The house keeps later hours when my Great Aunt comes visiting. I'll come then.'

For a moment stillness held all three of them; and then Tom Wildgoose said, 'Just like that? No questions asked?'

'No,' Peter said levelly.

'I could still be a spy.'

'I never thought you were. I thought we ought to make sure.'

Damaris began to feel that she was not there at all, and all this was between the two of them.

'And you're sure now?'

'Yes.'

'I wonder why?'

Peter pushed his fists into his pockets as though he would come out through the bottom of them. 'Damaris told me all that happened yesterday. If you had been a spy, I don't think you would have let them take you like that, *made* them take you. Not just for a vixen and the risk to a girl. Not if you were a good spy, worth your pay.'

'I could be a bad spy,' Tom suggested helpfully.

Peter grinned, 'There's that, of course. But if you were a spy, I reckon you'd be a middlin' good one.'

'My thanks,' said Tom. He seemed to be making up his mind about something, and when he spoke again, it was made up. 'All the same, I've the oddest feeling I should like you to know what's in that packet.'

'I'm quite content not to, unless you're sure, absolutely sure,' Peter said.

Damaris could have hit him.

Tom's hands that had been hanging lax across his knees, tightened into fists. 'I am sure. It's nothing so very important, anyway. Letters from the King's Court at St. Germaine to a handful of faithful followers of the cause—Prince Charles Edward's cause—in London.'

Damaris caught her breath, there was a feeling of cold shock in her. Nothing *important*! You—you're a Jacobite!'

Tom's face crinkled into its lopsided smile. 'So is your Aunt Selina, from what you have told me.'

'That's different. She's—she's not doing any harm, not carrying letters from the King's enemies.' Her voice was stunned and husky. 'Oh Tom, you *promised* me there was not anything that could hurt England or King George in that packet!'

'And that was the truth.' There seemed to be a sudden shadow over Tom's face, and the bitter brightness that she had seen before was in his eyes. 'Prince Charles had his chance five years ago—I was with him; my father, too, but my father died, like a good many more—he had his chance and he misused it, and he'll not get another. The Jacobite cause has loyal followers still, but it's a lost cause, Damaris.'

'Then why did you bring them, those letters? Why are you taking them through to London, as though they mattered?'

'Because those were my orders,' said Tom Wildgoose. 'Because—Oh I don't know. For a dream, maybe. . . . You don't stop serving the cause you were brought up in, just because it is lost.'

Peter, who was usually the sensible, down-to-earth one, said seriously, 'No, I can understand that.'

And looking at him, Damaris, still feeling oddly shaken, saw that he did, better in some ways than she could herself. Perhaps it was one of those things that men understood between themselves. Some men, anyway. And again, for that moment, she had the feeling of being shut out.

The trapdoor opened above their heads, and Genty's voice came down to them. 'Now then, up with 'ee, my lovers, 'tis time you were away to your homes afore there's more questions asked.'

'I'll leave *Don Quixote* with you,' Peter said, pulling the book from his pocket and laying it on top of a keg. 'Keep you company till I come back. Genty will keep it safe for me after you have done with it.'

He went up the ladder first, and behind him Damaris had just the one moment for a parting look back at Tom Wildgoose. Nothing had actually been said about his going that night, but suddenly she knew that if he could find any means of getting to Chichester, that was what he would do. And this was the last time she would see him. Cold desolation rose in her. Then Tom put that long forefinger under her chin, and tipped her face up very gently, and dropped a kiss, quick and light, on her forehead, and turned her firmly towards the ladder and Peter's disappearing heels.

Damaris rode home alone. There was no more reason now for Peter to escort her through the familiar woodlands, than there had been before Tom Wildgoose came, and anyway she did not want company just now, even Peter's. She could not help being just a little jealous of Peter, because for him the thing was not yet quite over: for him there was tonight's adventure still to come.

She thought of the two of them heading back through the dark woods to Joyous Gard, digging up for the sake of a lost cause the little oilskin packet from its place under the brambles, where it might just as well be left to lie forgotten. A ball of tears rose aching in her throat, and she rubbed the back of her hand angrily across her eyes.

As she did so, turning the fat pony out from the trees into the lane that led home, she heard the squeaking lilt of Shadow Mason's fiddle somewhere behind her—

'Farewell and adieu to ye fair Spanish Ladies,
Farewell and adieu to ye Ladies of Spain,
For we've received orders to sail for old
        England—'

The tune was growing fainter, fainter. . . . A turn in the lane brought it back for a moment.

'We'll rant and we'll roar li-like true British
        sailors,
We'll range and we'll rove far over salt seas. . . .

She just caught the familiar hiccup in the tune, and then the faint lilt was lost. He must have struck off down the track to Wittering, and the dense windbreak had cut off the sound.

There would be a cross on the stable door tonight. Well, it would not likely make any difference to Peter and Tom. The Fair Traders of the Manhood generally

ran their cargoes away southward, well beyond
Marsh Farm, or else on the far side, straight in from
the open Channel, hardly ever as far up towards the
harbour as this—too close under the eye of the Riding
Officers. If anyone had asked her how she knew, she
could not have told them: it was one of the things you
were born knowing, in the Manhood.

Chapter 12:
Voices in the Waggon Shelter

That afternoon Sukie had her kittens in a secluded corner of the granary, firmly ignoring the comfortable place that Caleb had made ready for her behind the chaff house. And at dusk, Damaris went to say goodnight to her and make sure that all was well with her and the kittens.

She went by way of the stable so that she could say goodnight to Snowball and the horses in passing. Earlier the stable would have been a busy place, with Daisy and Dolly and the rest being unharnessed and groomed clean of the day's mud that caked their feathered legs, and given their second feed of the day. But now Caleb and Dick would be away to their own places, and the only sound was the quiet stirring and soft puffing breaths of the teams, and a contented munching where Beauty was enjoying a mouthful of the sweet hay-straw that was in each horse's manger to last them through the night.

Damaris slipped from beast to beast with a pat in passing for each one. But she did not stop to fondle or talk to even Snowball. She would do that on the way back. No time now, for the light was going fast, and of course she could not take a lantern into the granary; and if she dawdled it would be too dark up there to see Sukie or the kittens properly.

At the far end of the stable a ladder led up into the hay-loft. Damaris gathered her skirts and scrambled up, and a few moments later she was in the granary by way of the hole where Caleb had removed a couple of boards to make things easier for himself when it came to refilling the corn bins.

In the granary the light was far gone, and the smell of the grain caught at her throat, and she would have been hard put to find the pile of old sacks where Sukie had made her nest, if she had not been there before, for the tiny stirring and whimpering was so faint that she could scarcely hear it until she was kneeling beside the nest. 'It's only me,' Damaris told the cat. 'Only me again.' Her fingers found the lean flank and then the velvet cap of fur between the pricked ears. Sukie turned her head sideways, pressing it up into the hollow of the caressing hand with a soft throaty purring in response.

A faint whiffling, a thread-thin sound of life came from the tiny squirming creatures along her flank. Very slowly and gently, Damaris picked up one after another, holding them high to catch the last pale light through the hoisting-window: one jet black like the wheelwright's tom, one pied like a wagtail, the rest faintly tiger-striped. Little ratlike creatures with blind groping mouths. But to Damaris they seemed almost as beautiful as they probably did to Sukie. She returned each one, careful to see that it was safely plugged in to its mother's milk, and remained for a while squatting contentedly beside them. Sukie's kittens always grew up to be splendid mousers, so there were always homes waiting for them, and none of them ever had to be drowned.

She was just beginning to think regretfully that it was time she went in for supper, when she realized that the faint rustling sounds of the granary were not the only ones she was hearing. Other sounds, small and stealthy, and above all, human, and men's low-pitched voices were seeping up through the floor from the waggon shelter below. Two men: one of them was Caleb, and there was nothing odd in that, he was often around the steading yard after he was off work for the night, and with a chalk cross on the stable door he would be at hand for sure. But there was that odd suggestion of stealth that was not like Caleb at all. And the other man—Damaris could never be sure in after years, but at the time she was almost sure that it was Luke Aylmer. And that did seem odd, for if the Big House bailiff was at Carthagena, she would have expected him to be talking with Father in the counting-house, not with Caleb Henty among the farm carts, and not in quite that way, either.

For there was something in the quick low growl of voices, that made her freeze into rigid stillness. It was not that she was eavesdropping, but that she was suddenly frightened, *very* frightened, of being caught seeming to eavesdrop. So she stayed, rather than risk a betraying move.

But soon she was straining to catch the muttered words, all the same.

'It may be just wild talk in the Black Horse taproom.' That was the man who sounded like Mr

Aylmer. 'But Daniel Cobby reckons 'tis true, and he's generally good enough at sifting the talk in his own taproom.'

'An' he reckons there's troops ordered down from Horsham to help t' Customs men?'

'Aye.'

Caleb cursed softly and fluently, 'So who's turned traitor on us?'

'Like enough nobody. That new Riding Officer at Selsey has more brains than are good for him.'

'Or us,' said Caleb. 'You reckon he's twigged?'

'I reckon at any rate that 'tis time Shadow Mason changed his tune. We've kept to the old code long enough. But that can wait: the mischief's done, and tonight's work is to undo it.'

'And how do us do that?'

'I've already arranged for the lugger to be signalled by flasher; we're switching the main cargo landing to Denman's Rife. I'm sending off a handful of the escort riders to Marsh Farm to make a diversion— give the troops and the customs men something to keep them busy.'

Caleb grunted in agreement; and there was a faint sound of movement below, as though the two men were on the edge of going their separate ways. And then Luke Aylmer's voice for the last time. 'Pass it on to the Birdham and Itchenor men when they come by.' And the faint movement again, fading into silence.

Damaris remained frozen into stillness, her ears straining after them through the silence until she was quite sure that they were really gone. Then she scurried back by the way she had come.

No time to talk to Snowball as she had intended. The white pony swung his head to stare after her in hurt surprise as she fled past. No time to spare for anything, with Tom and Peter heading straight into the Run, and maybe troopers loose in the woods as well, if the escort riders did not manage to draw them off. She must get to Genty's cottage quickly—quickly—and warn them. It was supper-time and yet again she would be missed, but there was no time to worry about that either.

She slipped in through the kitchen door, hoping to get by unnoticed in the preparations for supper, and fetch her cloak. It was turning cold with a mist beginning to creep in off the marshes, but it was not the cloak's warmth that she was thinking of, but it's darkness to cover her pale dress that might show up too clearly in the woods this evening. She slipped through and let the latch fall behind her—and was instantly pounced on by Hannah.

'And where have you been, my lady? I bin lookin' all over for you! Your Aunt's wantin' you.'

Damaris hovered on one foot. 'Is her headache worse?'

'No, no, she's better. Aye, sure-lye, an' talkin' about supper.'

'Oh good. Tell her how glad I am, Hannah—I'll just—' she was ready to fly, but found herself being bundled upstairs, all her protests and excuses seemingly unheard—and indeed what excuse could she make that would be worth listening to, and not betray Tom Wildgoose?—till she found herself in the big firelit, close-curtained chamber where Aunt Selina lay comfortably propped among her pillows like a stranded whale, and the door firmly shut behind her.

Aunt Selina's headache was certainly better. Her face, which had been yellowish-grey, was turning pink again amid the crisp white frills of her nightcap. She was beginning to feel like toying with a cold chicken leg and maybe a few cherry conserve tartlets, and beginning also to feel like company. So Damaris must needs take supper with her.

'It is all arranged,' she said, 'I dare swear your Father will not object to supping by himself for once, and Hannah will bring us up a tray. You will enjoy eating on a tray by the fire, and we shall be delightfully cosy.'

Once she had a moment to draw her breath and think straight, Damaris realized that her panic haste had really been quite needless. There was still around four hours left before Tom and Peter would be setting out from the Wise Woman's cottage. Plenty of time to warn them; and by not going until after supper she might even escape being missed. So she had her supper beside the fire—it took a long time, for Aunt Selina's idea of toying with a chicken leg and a few tartlets turned out to mean two trays laden with what looked to Damaris's despairing gaze to be half the contents of the larder. Her own insides were so cold and clenched with an odd mixture of fear and excitement that she did not want to eat anything at all, but she managed to nibble one of the chicken legs, so that Aunt Selina should not notice, and start wondering, as she always did if anyone around her showed signs of not being hungry, if they were sickening for something.

When at last supper was over, and Hannah had taken the trays away, she hoped she would be able to escape. 'Shall I move the candles? I expect you would like to sleep now, Aunt.'

But Aunt Selina did not feel in the least like sleeping. She waved vaguely towards the copy of The Gentleman's Magazine which lay on her dressing-table. The same copy of The Gentleman's Magazine did the round of half-a-dozen houses in the Manhood before it reached Carthagena, so it was at least three weeks out of date. But that did not really matter, for John Crocker seldom found time to do more than skim the overseas and political news, and the Court gossip, which Aunt Selina enjoyed (though always with a sigh because it was the Court of fat Hanoverian George, instead of the rightful King over the Water), was always, so far as Damaris could see, exactly the same.

'Read to me for a while, my dear,' said Aunt Selina. 'It will be improving for you to read of the Polite World, as well as being soothing for me, and I daresay we shall both sleep the better for the pleasant experience.'

Damaris swallowed a desperate protest. There was still time, of course, plenty of time, only—only she began to feel that the fire was much too hot, and the walls of the candlelit room were holding her prisoner, and with the heavy curtains drawn across the closed window, and the door fast shut she might not be able to hear the church clock or the little silvery one in the parlour, and so how was she to know what the time was?

She got up and fetched The Gentleman's Magazine, and returning to her seat, moved one of the candles nearer and turned to the Court and social pages, and began to read, breathlessly and rather fast, an account of a Court Ball at which the Princess of Wales had appeared in a sacque gown of sea-green paduasoy and a cap of the new style trimmed with point de Dunkerque lace.

'Not so fast, my love, anyone would think that you were running a race against time!' protested Aunt Selina.

Damaris drew a long breath, and started again, reading slowly and carefully. Maybe that would soothe Aunt Selina quickly off to sleep. But she read on and on, pausing only to snuff the candles, for a long time—or at least it seemed a long time—before a gentle snore from the bed told her that she was free to go, and she had long since used up all the Court and

Social news and droned her way through a long debate in Parliament and the advertisements for sporting guns and matched pairs of carriage horses, and the fire was sinking low.

She got up quietly, laid The Gentleman's Magazine back on the dressing-table, blew out one of the candles, and taking the dribbling stump that was all that remained of the other, stole out, closing the door softly behind her.

Looking down as she passed the head of the stairs she saw the line of light under the counting-house door, and that reminded her that she must bid goodnight to her father, lest, not having actually seen her all evening, he should look into her room on his way to bed, to make sure she was safely there. More delay! She put the candle on the top step, and ran downstairs. She tapped on the counting-house door which stood slightly ajar, and pushing it further open, went in.

Her father looked up from the farm ledger on the table before him. 'Not abed yet? You're late, Dimmy.'

Suddenly Damaris wished that she was not doing all these strange and lawless and exciting but rather frightening things without being able to tell him about them.

'Aunt would have me read to her after supper, and she has but this minute gone to sleep,' she said.

'So. And it's high time you were asleep too—close on ten o'clock.' He put an arm around her for a moment, rather absently, his attention still half on the ledger. 'Goodnight now. Happy dreams. Don't forget your prayers.'

Damaris dropped a kiss on the top of his ruffled brown head, 'Goodnight, Father. No, I won't.'

She fled back upstairs, collecting the guttering candle from the draughty stair-head, and a few moments later was back in her own bedroom, standing with her back to the door, heaving a long sigh of relief.

She did not say her prayers. There was no time.

She took her cloak from its place behind the door, and rolled it into a tight bundle tied with its own neck-strings. Then she blew out the candle and opened the window that gave onto the mulberry tree and the lane. Too dangerous to try leaving by the door, with Father still up and the household astir, and anyway the door would be barred against her when she got back. She waited a moment, listening. No sound from the stables: probably the Fair Traders had come for the horses while she was with Aunt Selina at the other side of the house.

She pulled a stool beneath the window, and climbed through onto the brewhouse roof. From the edge of the roof, she lobbed her bundled cloak through the mulberry branches towards the lane. It got as far as the tamarisk hedge, where it unfurled itself and hung scarecrow-fashion. No matter, it would be easy enough to collect in passing. She reached out, found the familiar mossy handhold and swung herself into the heart of the mulberry tree. She worked her way out along the further branch that dipped under her weight, and dropped into the lane.

Chapter 13: Wish on a Shooting Star

When she reached the Wise Woman's cottage there was no rush-light gleam in the window. She made her woodwind oyster-catcher call, and waited, listening for an answer. None came. She pushed the door open, and called softly, 'Genty? Genty?' Still nothing and no one answered her. The fire was banked for the night. Genty must be off about her own affairs, maybe with the sick baby again; and Tom and Peter must have set out already for Joyous Gard. If only Aunt Selina had not kept her so long reading The Gentleman's Magazine! Suddenly she realized as she had not quite done before, that in going to warn the other two, she was running into the same danger herself; and that it was quite possible, if the decoy riders failed in their task and she got caught between the smuggling band and the Troopers and Customs House men, that she might end up in the general confusion and the patchy mist, by getting herself shot.

Well, she would not get caught. She knew the woods better than the Customs men or any Troopers from Horsham, probably better than some of the smugglers did; and the alternative was to leave Tom and Peter to run into the danger unwarned.

She pulled her cloak more closely round her and turned back into the trees, heading straight for Joyous Gard, which was also straight for the Run. It was the third time that she had taken to the woods at night, and she was beginning to be used to the difference that came over familiar places when the dark came down upon them, changing shapes and sounds and distances from their daytime selves. But tonight there was another kind of strangeness abroad in the Manhood: the woods were awake and aware and hostile, a place where the crack of a twig might be a musket shot, and every bush or shadow or tree stump a crouching man. . . .

The mist that hung in faint ghostly swathes among the trees did not help, either, playing tricks with the direction of the sea-murmur, and more than once making Damaris think that she had lost the way. But at last she was at the spot where she had first found her smuggler lying face down among the roots of the oak tree. Only a little further now. She had taken such care to move quietly, but now despite herself she began to run. The little black hump that was Joyous Gard seemed to grow out of the mist to meet her, and away beyond it through the trees she caught the pale blurred glimmer of the Marsh. Somewhere out on the saltings where the mist eddied like smoke there was a moment's blink of light. The smugglers often used flint-and-steel for signalling, she knew; the light could carry half a mile on a clear night. Even tonight, as the faint mist wafted aside, she caught an answering blink from somewhere beyond the Rife, followed by a long-drawn whistling call.

In the same instant a shadow rose beside her, and a hand was over her mouth, and a voice whispered in her ear, 'Damaris! Don't make a sound!'

Cold terror leapt in her in the instant between the hand and the whispering voice, and was gone again as quick as the will-o'-the-wisp signal lights flashing along the Rife, for the voice was Tom's. She nodded against his hand to show that she understood, and he took it away. 'Good girl.'

She was crouching between two black shadows that were Tom and Peter, in the bramble patch against the old chimney-wall, looking out into the mist and the marsh and the faint dregs of moonlight. 'What in the world are you doing here?' Peter whispered in her other ear. 'There's a Run on.'

'I know. I heard Mr Aylmer talking to Caleb in the cart shelter. It was to have been out beyond Marsh Farm, but somebody got wind of it, and the Troopers are down from Horsham, so they moved the landing up here—Mr Aylmer said—and sent some escort riders down to Marsh Farm to—to act as decoys. They may be anywhere in the woods—so I came to warn you.'

'Thank you,' whispered Tom Wildgoose, politely.

'Have you got the packet?'

'Yes.'

'Then let's go! Let's go at once!'

'Not so fast—My means of getting to Chichester to catch the morning's stage is down there.' Her hood had fallen back, and Tom's breath tickled her ear.

'How?—What—'

'Look—there beyond the windbreak.'

The ancient thorn trees rising out of the drifting shore-mist had more than ever their witch-wife look; something stirred on the far side of them, and as the mist wafted back a little, Damaris saw a line of horses waiting for their riders or their loads of kegs.

'You can't! They'll have someone with them!'

'That's the problem,' Tom whispered back. 'This Mr Aylmer, he'll be the leader, by the sound of it. Who is he?'

'The Big House bailiff,' Peter told him.

'And you're sure it was him?'

Damaris nodded in the dark, 'Almost sure.'

There was a pause. Somewhere on the edge of hearing, a horse ruckled down its nose. Then Tom drew his legs under him. 'Have to risk it. Peter, you come with me; Damaris, you bide here. Don't move or make a sound. We'll be back as soon as maybe.'

The shadows on either side of her melted away, and she was alone in the shelter of the bramble patch.

The mist came and went in drifting swathes, and when it drifted close, blanketing sound as well as sight, she might have been alone in all the Manhood; and when it curled back on itself the waiting horses and the shapes of men hauling the bobbing porpoise-lines of kegs ashore, and the dip and creak of oars from boats hidden in the drifting paleness, seemed so close that she might have been in the very midst of all that was going forward.

Once a blue light flickered over to the right towards open water; once she heard the crack of a pistol somewhere in the woods Earnley way, which made her heart jump and race; once a horse squealed. Presently there began to be movement beyond the windbreak; pack-ponies being unhitched and led down the shore. She could hardly bear it, crouching there, straining for any sound that would tell her Tom and Peter had been discovered. She had no idea how time went by, but it seemed to be hours before there was a faint rustle on her right, and even as she tensed between fear and hope, Tom's voice whispered in her ear again, 'All's well. That didn't take long, did it?'

'Where's Peter?' she whispered back. 'Did you get a horse?'

'We did. Peter's waiting on the track with them. They're taking the pack beasts down now, and things are starting to move, so we'd best be moving, too.'

She got up and turned to follow him.

'You first,' Tom whispered, 'you're more sure of the way than I am.'

And she slipped past him and set off for the place where she always hitched Snowball. It seemed to her that Tom was making a lot of noise with his blackthorn staff, that would be because his knee was getting towards the end of what it could take, and anxiety grew in her, as well as the sharper fear of the men behind them. But they came safely to the old half-lost track, and found Peter waiting for them with his arm through the bridles of two saddle-horses.

'Why two?' she asked, stopping short.

'I'm going with Tom up to Chichester to bring his beast back,' Peter told her. 'Must obey the rules of the game—every borrowed horse safe back in its stable by morning. I can't quite manage that, but I can turn them loose on the Green, where they're sure to be found at first light.' He handed one of the horses over to Tom Wildgoose. 'Well, that all went quite smoothly, didn't it.'

Tom swung himself into the saddle, and Damaris heard him catch his breath with the pain and effort it cost him with his wounded knee. 'Quite smoothly,' he agreed, and tossed over his thorn staff for the other to carry. Then, to Damaris, he said, 'Give me your hand, and put your foot on mine; now—up with you.'

'Am I coming to Chichester, too?' asked Damaris in mid-flight. She had not been too happy waiting all alone at Joyous Gard with the Run going on as good as all around her; but to ride to Chichester on Tom's saddle-bow, that would be another thing altogether.

'No,' Tom said, dashing her hopes, 'we're taking you safe home on the way.' He flicked the reins and the horse moved forward, Peter riding close behind. 'But you'll have to tell me the way.'

'How did you steal the horses?' she asked after a little while, settling herself more comfortably into the crook of his bridle arm.

'Borrow,' Tom corrected. 'Simply told the horse-holders that Mus' Aylmer wanted two of the saddle-horses over at Marsh Farm—Then I wondered if I should not have used his name, but I didn't know what else to call him—Didn't seem to make any difference.'

There was a tight-drawn note in his voice, and Damaris felt how he held himself stiff and a little sideways in the saddle, and she knew that his knee must be hurting him, and held back from asking any more questions, scarcely speaking at all, except now and then to tell him the way.

Just before the old track turned them over to the lane, he reined in and sat listening. From away down the lane seaward came the sound of hooves, many hooves, like a pack-train on the move but without the clonk of bells that always announced a pack-train to other users of the road. The first of the newly landed cargo on its way to the hides. Tom and Peter urged their horses back into the underbrush, and waited.

The hoof-beats came nearer; now they were only just beyond the bend of the lane, and up the little rise came the black shapes of horsemen: the fore-riders of the train, and then the train itself, plodding, jogging along under their slung kegs and bales, with men either side, afoot or moving to and fro on horseback along their line. The lane was full of the ragged clippety-clop of hooves and the creak of harness leather.

Damaris felt the horse shift under her. What if he whinnied in greeting as horses do at the nearness of their own kind? Her breath stopped and she felt Tom's arm tighten round her.

But the dark train passed safely until even the rear-riders following after, were gone. The smother of hoof-beats died away, and the lane was quiet as before.

Tom heeled his horse forward again out of the woodshore. 'Which way, Honey?'

Damaris had for the moment forgotten that she was his pilot. 'Right, here . . . Now left—take to the driftway just beyond the big willow . . .' And soon after, they were in Carthegena Lane. They went quietly, keeping to the grass verge to muffle the sound of hoof-beats, until rounding the last corner, there was the dark peaceable shape of the old house sleeping companionably among its huddle of out-buildings.

'That's home,' Damaris said, and seeing no lights in the windows, nor any sign of a stir, heaved a sigh of relief. She had not been missed.

'What about dogs?' Tom whispered, reining in to a walk.

'They won't make any noise, not when there's a Run on.'

'So, all's well. Now how do we get you in?'

'Here,' said Damaris. 'The mulberry tree.'

He brought the horse to a halt below the great branch that arched out into the lane. 'Can you manage that way?' he asked doubtfully.

'I've come and gone by it often enough before.'

'Right, then,' his hold shifted and his hands were on either side of her waist. 'Up with you! Stand on the saddle-bow. I have you safe—'

She scrambled up and was among the branches almost without having to reach for them. She gained her feet on the main branch, and stood up, finding a familiar handhold. The two in the lane looked a long way down.

Peter's hoarse whisper came up through the twig-tangle, 'I'll be over first thing in the morning to give Sim Bundy a hand in the lambing fold.'

'Yes, you come,' said Damaris, but she was looking at Tom Wildgoose standing in his stirrups just below her. 'Goodbye, Tom.' It sounded foolish and polite in her own ears, like saying goodbye to someone who had been to drink chocolate with Aunt Selina, but there was an ache inside her not quite like anything that she had ever felt before.

'Goodbye, Damaris,' Tom said. 'Now in with you. I'll wait to see you safely through the window.'

And she knew that she must not delay them. Every moment was dangerous. She shifted her hold and moved back, changed branches, and was standing on the brewhouse roof. Her window was open just as she had left it. She hitched up her skirts and scrambled through, turning the instant her feet touched the floor, to lean out again. Through the bare mulberry branches she could see the two dark shapes waiting in the lane. Tom's upturned face was a pale blur in the darkness: he put up his hand in a wide leave-taking salute; and as she waved in reply, urged his horse forward, Peter after him, hooves almost soundless on the grass verge.

Behind them the lane was left empty. This time it really was over.

The mist was clearing, though it still clung wispily

along the ground. The young moon was long since down, but looking up, Damaris could see the stars; the same stars she had counted on the night that it all began. She gazed up at them, seeing them blurred and fuzzy with her own sudden weariness. She had not known that it was possible to be so tired. . . .

And it was in that moment, as she fumbled with the neck-strings of her cloak, almost as she turned towards her bed, that she saw the shooting star. The far-travelling arrow–point of light that seemed to spring clear of the topmost mulberry branches, high overhead, and arch out over the Manhood. She had wished on a shooting star often enough in the winter, but you did not often see one so late into the edge of spring. That must surely make it all the more special, all the more potent for wishing on.

Watching it until it disappeared above the rim of trees at the world's edge, Damaris wished with all the strength of wishing that was in her, not for a flame-coloured petticoat, this time, but that all should be well with Tom Wildgoose on his road to London, and through all his years to come.

Five years went by, and then the half of another year, and on a soft blustery September evening, Damaris and Peter came back from a walk together. Earlier, they had been at the Vicarage, talking over some plans for their wedding in a fortnight's time. The weeks between harvest and the start of the autumn ploughing, when the farming year drew breath, was always a favourite time for weddings among farming folk.

Peter's father had not been over-pleased at Peter's determination to turn farmer rather than follow him into the Church. But with Carthegana lacking a son to follow on when John Crocker grew too old to farm it, he had had to admit in the end that it was really a very sensible arrangement.

After the Vicarage, they had called on Genty Small to make sure that she was coming to the wedding, and then on a sudden whim they had turned out of their way to go round by the little lost cottage in the woods. They had not been there for a long while, and they had found scarcely anything left of Joyous Gard but the doorsill and the remains of the hearth, and a few rotten timbers lost among the brambles.

'It makes me feel quite old and rather sad,' Damaris had said, and Peter had laughed at her, and they had gone on their way.

But going so far out of their road had made them later than they meant to be. Also the sight of the old cottage had started them off saying, 'Do you remember—?' which is always a thing to make people walk slowly, and sunset was flying like golden banners all across the levels of the Manhood as they came in through the autumn tangle of the garden towards the kitchen door.

'I was never more thankful for anything than I was when I got down to the lambing fold next morning and found you safely there and no harm come to you or Tom,' Damaris was saying. Their talk on the way through the woods had made it all seem so close, as though it had happened only yesterday. And yet in another way it was so long ago. She had been only twelve then, and now she was seventeen, going on eighteen—quite old and getting married.

Sukie lay in the last warmth of the day beside the brushwood pile, suckling her latest kittens. She was getting to be a little stiff in the joints but her kittens still grew up to be the best mousers in Manhood.

Damaris stooped to stroke her, and so glimpsed a flat parcel wrapped in oilskin lying half-hidden among the brushwood. She parted the sticks a little, and saw carefully painted on the oilskin

'Mistress Damaris Crocker, for her wedding'

'What is it?' asked Peter behind her.

'I don't know. A wedding-present for me, seemingly.'

But she did know. Memory was twinging in her, even as the pulled the package from its half-hiding place, and turned, holding it in her arms.

The knots in the tarred string were stiff to undo, and Peter, though he hated wasting string, fished in his pocket for his knife and cut them for her. Under the stiff folds of oilskin was a covering of calico. And inside the calico, as she turned that back also—she let out a little gasp of delight as the sunset fell upon glowing folds of flame-coloured taffeta that seemed to echo its own fires.

Fold upon fold spilled out across her arm. 'Careful!' Peter said, 'You'll get it muddy'—even as she swooped to gather up the loose end before it could touch the ground.

There was no letter—she knew that there would not be—just the painted direction on the oilskin. 'Mistress Damaris Crocker, for her wedding.' He had promised, and he had kept his promise.

With the glowing mass that was the very colour of joy gathered into her arms, she turned to Peter. Square, dependable Peter, with the square, dependable face.

'Will you marry me in a flame-coloured taffeta petticoat, if I promise to keep it well hidden under my wedding-dress?'

'You don't need to promise anything,' Peter said. 'I'll marry you in any petticoat you please!' And flung his arms round her, laughing, and hugged her close.